KT-499-659

Hot Rock Mountain

Elizabeth Laird

EGMONT

For William

First published in Great Britain 2004
by Egmont Books Limited
239 Kensington High Street, London W8 6SA

Text copyright © 2004 Elizabeth Laird
Illustration copyright © 2004 Bill McConkey

The moral rights of the author and illustrator have been asserted

ISBN 1 4052 0324 2

1 3 5 7 9 10 8 6 4 2

A CIP catalogue record for this title is available from the British Library

Typeset by Avon DataSet Ltd, Bidford on Avon, Warwickshire B50 4JH
Printed and bound in Great Britain by the CPI Group

This paperback is sold subject to the condition that it shall not, by way of trade or otherwise,
be lent, resold, hired out, or otherwise circulated without the publisher's prior consent in any
form of binding or cover other than that in which it is published and without a similar
condition including this condition being imposed on the subsequent purchaser.

Hot Rock Mountain

Elizabeth Laird was born in New Zealand but she lived in London until she grew up. As soon as she could, she began to travel, and went off to live first in Malaysia, then in Ethiopia, Iraq, Lebanon and Austria. Now she lives near London with her husband, who is also a writer, and her two sons. She likes reading (a lot), gardening, walking, going to the cinema, talking to friends and cooking (sometimes). Her books have won and been nominated for many awards, including the Carnegie Medal and the Smarties Award.

Also by Elizabeth Laird

Contents

Foreword

The stories in this book picture the natural world, in all its diversity. The long ones I wrote from my own imagination, but the short stories come from many different countries and traditions. They've been told for centuries – some of them for thousands of years. They link the longer stories, like small beads on a necklace of larger ones. I chose to include them because they're interesting, or beautiful, or because I've known them and loved them for a long time. Their meanings match the themes in this book.

Most of my own stories come out of places I've visited and things I've seen in my travels.

'Hot Rock Mountain' (the mountain is really a volcano, of course) was inspired by a visit to Stromboli, a thrilling live volcano on an island near Italy. I climbed it once on a dark night, with my children, and saw red hot lava shooting up out of it into the sky. On the island next to Stromboli we rolled about in warm mud and washed it off afterwards in the steaming hot sea.

Snakes are scary creatures. I should know. I was bitten by one once in the South China Sea, and I nearly died. Years later, a black mamba dropped out of a tree a few metres from where I stood in a forest in Southern

Ethiopia. It gave me the shudders, but I was thrilled too. Snakes may be dangerous to humans, and mysterious in their ways, but there's no reason why we should persecute them. Their right to life is as great as ours, and that's why I wrote 'Black Mamba'.

'Long Wing' was written after I'd sailed down the Otago Sound, in New Zealand, and watched the great Royal Albatrosses, with their two-metre wing spans, coming in to land on the rocky headlands after their thousand-mile flights over and around the vast southern oceans of the world. I learned later of the sad fate that awaits many of them.

'Lord of the Garden' reminds me of a summer night in France. The honey-coloured stones of the ancient courtyard where I sat were warm after a day's sun. Bats were flying overhead and bull frogs chorused from the pond nearby. Suddenly, with a startling screech, an owl flew out from the church belfry overhead and flitted, a white shadow, over the hedgerows to hunt in a farm yard nearby, where hidden dangers lurked.

In 'Mr Hasbini's Garden', I recalled life in Beirut during the terrible civil war. In the middle of all the fear and destruction, the bombings and shootings and terror, I watched with wonder as nature reclaimed the ruined city. Young trees began to grow up through the smashed tarmac and wild flowers sowed themselves in the nooks of shattered walls.

'Skippy' is a story about the fate of exotic pets. I didn't

know anything about the cruel traffic in smuggled animals until I visited the Animal Reception Centre at the back of Heathrow Airport. I saw some of the many frightened, lonely, rare and endangered creatures that have been trapped in the wild and brought into Europe to be sold to humans as their playthings.

The mineral world is seen in 'Why the Sea is Salty'. This story comes from Ethiopia, a country sadly afflicted by famine, but rich in wonderful tales that have been passed down through many generations. I've travelled to the farthest corners of that beautiful land in search of stories, and all kinds of people – teachers, nuns, farmers, merchants, priests, camel drivers, bards, students and even a prison governor – have told me the tales their grandmothers told them.

I wish I could say that the sight of an otter in the wild had inspired 'Coming Home', but like most people I never have seen one. Otters are so shy and secretive that they rarely let themselves be glimpsed. All you're likely to see is a webbed footprint in wet mud. But as I've tramped through Scottish glens and along East Anglian streams, I'm willing to bet that some time, somewhere, a hidden otter's bright black eyes have watched me pass by.

The stories in this book share a common theme. They celebrate nature, and the creatures among whom we humans live, but they sound some warnings too. Humankind has become too powerful in the last few centuries. We have swept all other species aside in our greed, and destroyed much that is rare and beautiful.

We have to realise what we're doing. We have to stop and think.

Acknowledgements

Many people and organisations have helped in the research for this book. I would like to thank:

Stephen Spawls, co-author of *The Dangerous Snakes of Africa*, for his help with 'Black Mamba'.

Euan Dunn of the Royal Society for the Protection of Birds for his help with 'Long Wing'.

Mr Hasbini, whose garden I often visited in Beirut.

Charles Mackay of the CITES Enforcement Team, and the staff at the Animal Reception Centre at Heathrow Airport for the inspiration for 'Skippy'.

The Hawk and Owl Trust for help with 'Lord of the Garden'.

Richard Sheuter of the Otter Trust in Earsham, Suffolk, for his help with 'Coming Home'.

The folk tales, myths and legends in the book were retold from the following sources:

'The Message in the Thunder' from *Myths and Legends of India*, William Radice, Folio Society, 2001.

'The Goddess and the Snake', from *The Greek Myths* by Robert Graves, first published by Penguin Books, 1955.

'The Flood' from the Bible.

'Ninurta and Kur', a Mesopotamian–Sumerian story first transcribed in 2,000 BC. From *Myths of the World* by Michael Jordan, Kyle Cathie Ltd, 1993.

'The Crocodile and the Cassowary Bird' from *New Guinea Folk Tales* by Brenda Hughes, George G. Harrap and Co Ltd, 1959.

'The Bear and the Woman', narrated to Elizabeth Laird by Abdisa Labe in southern Ethiopia.

'The Most Precious Thing' from *Household Tales, with Other Traditional Remains Collected in the Counties of York, Lincoln, Derby and Nottingham*, Sidney Oldall Addy, London and Sheffield, 1895.

'Why the Sea is Salty' from *Teret Teret*, ed. by Brian Wilks, published 1971, printed by Central Printing Press, Addis Ababa.

'Deep Sea and Dry Land' from *The Orchard Book of Creation Stories* by Margaret Mayo, illustrated by Louise Brierley, Orchard, 1995.

If you would like to find out more about some of the subjects these stories touch on, here are a few websites you might like to check out.

The Otter Trust – www.ottertrust.org.uk

The Hawk and Owl Trust – www.hawkandowl.co.uk

The Royal Society for the Protection of Birds – www.rspb.org.uk

The Reptile Trust – www.reptiletrust.com

The Message in the Thunder

An ancient story from India

At the beginning of time, the Creator, Brahma, made gods, people and demons.

The demons were greedy and violent. They murdered and stole, grabbing what they could. But the riches they gained did not bring them happiness. The demons were restless and dissatisfied. They realised that all was not well with them, and decided to go to Brahma, their Creator, to ask his advice.

The people were not happy either. They were clever, and made many things, but they quarrelled jealously over their possessions and each person tried to become rich at the expense of others. They, too, decided to return to Brahma and ask for his help.

The gods should have been contented in their far-off heaven. They lived in pleasure and luxury, with beautiful nymphs to serve them. They had magical powers at their command, so that they could turn themselves into any shape that took their fancy. But none of this brought them happiness and they went to seek out Brahma, too.

Brahma was resting when the beings he had created stood in front of him and said, 'Oh Grandfather, please tell us how we can be happy, and find peace.'

Only one word came forth from Brahma. It was a huge

sound, a deafening cry. It rolled round the universe, louder than a gigantic clap of thunder.

'DA!' he roared.

Then he closed his eyes and returned to his peaceful meditation.

The demons returned to their underworld, the people to earth, and the gods to heaven, to think about what Brahma had said.

The gods decided that 'da' must be short for 'damyata', which means 'to be self-controlled'.

'Our Creator has told us not to spend all our time in idle pleasures,' they said, 'but to restrain ourselves. That way lies our happiness.'

The people thought that 'da' meant 'datta', which means 'to give'.

'We should be generous to each other,' they said, 'and care less about possessions. The earth is for all living creatures, not only for ourselves. We must share it with them.'

The demons took longest to decide on the meaning of the Creator's cry, but at last they agreed that 'da' meant 'dayadhvam', which means 'to be merciful'.

'We should treat those in our power with kindness,' they told each other, 'and refrain from cruelty.'

These lessons are hard to learn and are often forgotten. And that is why the thunder rolls out from time to time across the universe, as the Creator repeats his message.

Hot Rock Mountain

Tad Mulcaster was the richest boy in the world. He lived in an amazing house with twenty bedrooms, a huge swimming pool, two games rooms, five garages and a deer park, and he had his own car (with driver) and even his own helicopter (with pilot).

Nobody liked Tad much, except for his mother, but she didn't see him often because she was too busy shopping. He only had one friend, Matthew, whose mum was Tad's housekeeper. Matthew lived in a poky little flat above the garages and hung out with Tad because there was no one else.

Tad's father had gone off years ago with a film star, but Tad's granddad was still around. He spent all day in a very small office at the top of a skyscraper, in the heart of the world's richest city, crouched like a giant spider over a desk the size of a ping-pong table, and made money. Lots of money.

'It's my birthday today,' Tad said gloomily to Matthew one morning.

'Great,' said Matthew. He wasn't really listening because he was playing a brilliant game on one of Tad's four computers.

'I *said*,' said Tad, 'it's my *birthday*.'

'Right,' said Matthew. 'What do you reckon you'll get?'

Tad shrugged.

'Dunno. Mum's away at the fashion shows, and Dad never remembers. Unless *you've* got something for me. Have you? *Have* you?'

'Sorry,' Matthew said, looked round at Tad a little nervously. 'Look, I meant to get you a CD, but you've got all the ones you like already. I was going to ask you what you wanted and get it for you. Honest.'

'I see,' said Tad, frowning.

He leaned over Matthew and pressed Escape. The computer game was wiped out.

'Hey!' said Matthew indignantly. 'I was doing really well!'

'Whose computer is it?' Tad said nastily. 'Did I say you could use it? *Did* I?'

'No,' said Matthew, 'but . . .'

Tad wasn't listening. He had opened up his email.

'Looks like there's something from Granddad,' he said, sounding surprised. He read the message out.

'Dear grandson, my secretary tells me it's your

4

birthday. I have a gift for you. It's a mountain called Hot Rock Mountain, and my experts tell me that it's an interesting investment. See what you can do with it. Many happy returns. Granddad.'

'A mountain! Wow!' Matthew's mouth had fallen wide open. Tad was already holding his phone to his ear.

'Pilot's on stand-by. Let's go.'

'Us?' asked Matthew, turning green. 'You and me? No thanks. I'm not that keen on flying, to be honest.'

'You want to be my friend or not?' demanded Tad.

'Yeah, I suppose so.'

'Then shut up and do what I tell you.'

Two hours later, Tad and Matthew stepped out of Tad's helicopter on to a beach with sand so fine and white that it felt to Matthew like silk under his feet. The clean warm sea, its water a transparent pale green shot through with blue, lapped towards their feet, leaving behind with each wave a harvest of perfect pink shells.

'Stay here!' Tad yelled to the pilot, over the roar of the helicopter's engine. 'We're going to explore.'

The pilot put his thumbs up and smiled, but under his breath he said, 'And I hope you never come back, you spoiled brat.'

Then he cut the engine, leaned back in his seat, and closed his eyes for a snooze.

Tad and Matthew looked up at the mountain. It rose straight up from the beach. The top was bare and circled by a ring of cloud, which floated around it like a crown of cotton wool. The lower slopes were covered with trees, some decked with scarlet flowers, some dripping with golden globes of fruit. Now that the engine sound had died away, the songs of a thousand birds could be heard.

Tad stood with his hands on his hips, gazing up at his mountain, measuring it with his eyes.

An interesting investment, he thought. I reckon Granddad could be right.

'Up there,' he said, pointing. 'That's where the holiday complex will be. And that's where it'll start.'

'What'll start?' asked Matthew, squinting up against the brilliant sunshine.

'The rollercoaster. The most amazing one the world has ever seen.' Tad's hands were flying about, swooping and diving as the gigantic rollercoaster took shape in his mind.

'Wow,' said Matthew, impressed. Then he shook his head. 'But it would take too long to get up there, every time you wanted a go.'

'Are you an idiot or just a total fool?' demanded Tad. 'There'll be a cable car of course. Starting from right here.'

Matthew shook his head again.

'You couldn't have a cable car. It would get all tangled up in the trees.'

Tad dismissed the trees with a wave of his hand.

'I'm having them cut down. And that bit over there' – he pointed across to the right – 'that's where the computer game complex will be.'

'You've got four computers already. Isn't that enough?' Matthew said drily.

'I don't mean actual computers. This is going to be like a whole virtual world. I'll be able to get right inside and run through the game myself, and it'll be like it's really happening all around me. I'm going to get the experts on to it.'

Matthew frowned.

'You can't do that, Tad. It's not safe. Computer games are deadly dangerous. There's loads of smash-ups and people getting wasted and stuff.'

'It'll be safe for *me*,' boasted Tad.

'Yeah, but you have to have people to chase, and shoot at. Who's going to want to do that?'

Tad stared at him.

'You are, of course.'

Matthew laughed.

'You've got to be kidding,' he said, but he gave Tad a long look, and when Tad wasn't looking, raised his eyebrows and rolled his eyes.

Tad didn't notice. He was pointing to the left.

'And over there, that's where I'll put my main house, and a massive swimming pool with slides and stuff.'

'Slides are stupid,' said Matthew. 'What's wrong with just going in the sea?'

'Who asked you? Whose place is this, anyway?'

'Oh yours, Tad. It's yours.' Matthew was staring

7

into the trees. 'Wow, listen to those birds.'

'They do my head in.' Tad stuck his fingers in his ears and wiggled them about. 'I'm going to wire the whole place up with loudspeakers that'll play my favourite music. Come on. What are we waiting for?'

He set off towards the fringe of trees, whose glossy crowns of bright green leaves shimmered gently in the scented breeze.

Matthew didn't move. He was looking up at the mountain with awe in his eyes.

'If it was anyone but Tad,' he said out loud, 'I'd think he was just kidding, but knowing him, he means it.'

Suddenly, he felt something odd underfoot, a sort of quivering, as if the sand was gently shaking. It was as if he was standing on a bowl of jelly.

'Tad!' he called after him, but Tad was already out of sight. He'd found a path between the trees and was following it.

It was the sort of path that seemed to have made itself. It wandered through the tree trunks, bending politely round the flowering bushes, sloping gently upwards all the time. Humming birds flitted round Tad's head but he didn't notice them. Small furry creatures with gem-like eyes watched him silently from the cracks in the rocks and the branches overhead but he had no idea they were there.

The path was getting steeper. It seemed now more like a stairway, roughly hewn out of the rock. Tad looked up, putting a hand on a nearby boulder to steady himself.

'The cable car can start from here,' he muttered out loud. 'I'll have them concrete all this bit over and – ouch!'

He had suddenly realised that the stone he was touching was hot. Very hot. So hot that it was burning his fingers. He snatched his hand away.

Weird, he thought. Why on earth . . .?

A noise from above made him look up. A monkey with a black and white face was sitting on a branch above his head, eating nuts and throwing down the shells.

'Hey! Mind where you're throwing that stuff!' shouted Tad. 'Who do you think you are? First thing I'll do is make some cages and have you locked up.'

Matthew had followed him.

'Why on earth would you lock up the monkeys? They're doing OK up there in the trees. I think they're great.'

'They chucked stuff at me!' said Tad indignantly. 'Anyway, they're wild animals. They might bite me and give me rabies and stuff.'

Matthew shook his head, but Tad had already started climbing again.

'Come on! Keep up!' Tad said impatiently.

He was beginning to get out of breath. He had almost decided to go down again and order the helicopter pilot to fly them to the summit of the mountain, when he reached the top of the rocky stairway. The path broadened and flattened out here, and he found himself in a little clearing in the forest. Blue and white flowers spangled the grass and clusters of ripe wild strawberries made scarlet dots among their serrated leaves.

'This is where I'm going to put my roller rink,' Tad said.

Matthew looked up.

'Tad, are you crazy? You could build a roller rink anywhere. This place is special. Why mess it up?'

Tad wasn't listening. He'd stepped back to get a better view of the glade.

'The ground's flat enough here. We just need to get rid of all the jungle, and blast out the rock on that side . . . Hey!'

He'd suddenly realised that the ground he was standing on was soft. Very soft. So soft that he was sinking into it. He leaped forward again, on to solid stone.

'Concrete'll sort this lot out,' snarled Tad. 'Sooner I get them started on it the better.'

Matthew was shaking his head. He looked disgusted.

'I don't want to listen to this. You're going to wreck the place. Cutting down the trees, banging up the monkeys, concreting everything over – it's stupid. It's pathetic. It's horrible.'

Tad stared at him. He wasn't used to being argued with. He was used to doing exactly what he liked, and forcing everyone else to do it too. His face went red with anger.

'Shut up!' he yelled. 'Get off my mountain! Call yourself my friend? I don't know why I've stuck with you all this time. Anyone else would be *proud* to be my friend. They'd *love* to be my friend. Have you forgotten that I'm the richest boy in the world?'

'Forgotten?' snorted Matthew. 'How could I forget, with you ramming it down my throat every five minutes? You're a creepy little slimeball, Tad, and you can keep your helicopter and your mountain.'

Tad was speechless with astonishment.

'And there's another thing.' Matthew put out a finger and stabbed Tad's chest with it. 'This mountain's not going to do what you want, either. It's fantastic, this place is. It won't let you muck it up. There's weird stuff going on, or hadn't you noticed? Hot rocks, squidgy ground, sand like jelly, and this funny smell I keep getting. Like rotten eggs or something.'

Tad had gone rather limp in the middle, but now he straightened himself up.

'Rotten eggs?' he yelped. 'Rotten *eggs*? On *my* mountain? How dare you? No one's ever spoken to me like that before. It's not allowed. Not to *me.*'

Tad backed away from Matthew, turned, ran off out of the glade, and began climbing fast through the trees up the side of the mountain.

He was so angry that he didn't notice that the trees were thinning out and that he was emerging into an open space. Sunlight hitting his face made him look up, and he saw that he was standing at the edge of a small lake. Clouds of steam were blowing off it, rising into the air like billows of smoke, and the water was erupting all over the surface, as if it was actually boiling.

Tad stepped forward. A plopping, gurgling sound made him look down. The mud at the edge of the lake was moving! Big grey bubbles of it were blowing themselves up, then popping loudly and sinking down again. He stepped back. He could feel the heat coming off the hot mud and the steaming lake and it scared him.

'I'm going to change all this,' he said out loud, trying not to sound doubtful. 'I'm going to get rid of all this stinking mud and get them to cool the water down and make this into a jacuzzi. Then I'll . . .'

Suddenly, with a violent whoosh and a deafening roar, a huge jet of water and steam spouted up in the middle of the lake. Drops of searing water from the massive fountain splashed on to Tad's face, and the pain of it made him stumble backwards.

He didn't see the precipice falling away behind him. He knew nothing about it until he felt emptiness under his feet, and began to fall. Wildly, he clutched at the air, and hit the ground at last. Here he lay, quite sure that he was dead, with his eyes tight shut.

After a while he opened them again, sat up and looked round. He'd landed on a mound of soft moss and hadn't hurt himself at all. Beside him was a little pool. Trees grew all around, but shafts of sunlight shone through to glisten on the wet rocks. A waterfall, spilling down the cliff face, splashed into the pool and brilliant blue dragonflies darted through the spray. Flowers like flame-coloured trumpets grew by the pool's edge and tiny birds, as bright as jewels, hovered in front of them, sipping nectar through their long beaks. The sulphurous, rotten smell had gone, and instead Tad could smell fruit, something ripe and delicious, something succulent and tempting.

He almost wanted to explore, to hunt for the fruit and eat it, but he was still too angry, and shaken by his fall. He staggered to his feet, looked into the pool, and caught sight of his own face.

It was nothing but a little round blob in the water, grey coloured and insignificant. Behind it he could see vast mirrored trees, and the cliff down which he'd fallen, and the steam from the lake, drifting across the sky. For the first time in his life, he felt small and unimportant.

'This is stupid,' he said loudly. 'This can't be happening to *me*.'

Almost as if the mountain had heard him, an answering rumble came from somewhere deep below his feet.

Tad realised, all of a sudden, that he was quite alone.

'Matthew,' he called out uncertainly. 'Where are you?'

The only answer was a cacophony of squawking as a flock of bright green parrots settled in the trees overhead and began pecking at the fruit.

'Matthew!' Tad called again. 'Are you there? I didn't mean it about chasing you around in the computer game. Honestly.'

His voice echoed back at him off the rocks.

'There's got to be a way down from here,' muttered Tad. He began to stumble about over the uneven ground, but the hollow into which he'd fallen, with its pool and its fruit trees, its waterfall and its dragonflies, was walled in by cliffs on all sides. The only gap was where the stream cascaded out, down and down over another precipice, on to rocks miles below.

This is really stupid, Tad thought incredulously. I can't be trapped, not on my own mountain.

Frantically, he began to explore the hollow again. It was no good. The cliffs were too sheer to climb and the gap, through which the stream was falling, was much too steep and slippery to follow. There was no way out at all. He was stuck.

'Matthew!' Tad called again, in a quavering voice. 'Help!'

But he knew it was no good. Matthew had gone forever. Tad went back to the pool and flopped down on to a rock.

They'll come for me soon, he told himself. They'll search the whole place. My pilot, he'll come and look for me.

But he remembered the flash of dislike he'd half noticed in the man's eyes.

Mum and Granddad, they wouldn't leave me stuck here.

But Grandad had never been known to leave the city, and as for Mum, she was at the fashion shows.

My chauffeur, one of the staff, my – my dad, he

thought. Surely one of them would . . .

But he wasn't sure at all. He was suddenly overwhelmed with self-pity.

It's no good, he thought. Nobody cares about me. No one will mind if they ever see me again or not.

A tear ran down his cheek, then another and another. They splashed on to the rock beside him. Something else had landed beside him too. A big yellow mango, falling from the tree overhead, had plopped down on to a soft bed of moss right next to his hand. Tad picked it up and held it to his nose. Without thinking what he was doing he'd torn the skin off with his teeth and had started to eat the flesh.

When he'd finished he felt a little better. He hadn't realised how hungry he was.

A splash in the pool made him look round. A small frog had jumped out of it and was squatting on a floating leaf. And above its head was a banana tree, with a big bunch of ripe yellow bananas just within Tad's reach.

He leaned over and picked a couple. He didn't eat much fruit usually, but these bananas were delicious. No, more than delicious. They were sensational!

Eating had made Tad thirsty. He usually drank nothing but Coke, but the water looked so cool and fresh he couldn't resist trying it. He scooped some up into his cupped hands and drank. It tasted wonderful.

He looked round the hollow again.

'It's nice here,' he mused aloud. 'Maybe you were

right, Matthew. Maybe I wouldn't change this bit, not the trees, and the pool and everything. And perhaps I'll let the monkeys and birds and stuff stay here too.'

Again there came a faint, faint rumble from somewhere inside the mountain, but this time, instead of sounding angry, it was almost like a purr.

Tad frowned.

Maybe there is something weird here. It's almost as if the mountain's trying to tell me something. Those hot rocks, I only felt them when I said that stuff about cutting down trees for a cable car. The ground went soft only when I was telling Matthew I'd make a roller rink. Yes, and then that fountain up there boiled all over me when I was thinking out loud about a giant jacuzzi. I'll try it out.

He stood up and said loudly, 'Are you listening, mountain? I'm going to build a factory right here and put all the stream water into bottles and sell it. Did you hear me? Oh! *Oh*!'

A cloud of choking yellow gas had suddenly rolled down the cliff towards him. It filled his nose with the most disgusting stink, then it rolled on through the gap in the rock wall and fell like the water down the waterfall.

'Phew,' said Tad, who'd been almost knocked flat. 'Wow. It's true then. This mountain's alive. It can hear me! It talks!'

He cleared his throat.

'OK,' he said, a bit nervously. 'I'll forget all the other stuff, but how do you feel about me blasting away just a little bit of rock around here so I can build myself a nice house? Just asking. No need to go – hey, stop that! It's all right! I won't!'

A shower of stones had detached itself from the cliff and was rattling down all around him.

'Well,' said Tad, thinking hard. 'I expect this is an idea you'll love. I bet you like wildlife, what with the monkeys and the birds and everything. What if I put a fence all the way around and make a wildlife park? Some more monkeys, you know, those funny ones with red bottoms, and a few scary things like bears and leopards and stuff. Tourists would love it. We'd have helicopter tours – it would only need one little helicopter pad – No? Wow, that was some rumble you gave out there. OK, no wildlife park. So what do you want?'

The silence was suddenly total. For a moment, not even the wind rustled the leaves, no birds were singing and even the water flowed in silence.

'Nothing? You want nothing? You want me to leave you exactly as you are?' Tad was amazed. 'But don't you understand? This place is a goldmine! If you don't want me to do stuff just for myself, think of the money we could make! The tourists! The beach itself is worth a fortune! I'd spend all the money on improvements, honestly I would. New paths, a visitors centre, decent cages for the monkeys . . .'

A ferocious grinding, crashing sound from below nearly rocked him off his feet. He sat down.

'Nothing,' he said. 'You just want to be left alone, is that it? You want to go on being exactly the way you are?'

A thought occurred to him.

'You don't mind if I come here sometimes though, do you? To visit? Just to wander round and take a look at things? With Matthew, if he and I are ever friends again?'

The parrots, who had been feeding quietly in the trees, took off suddenly and wheeled round Tad's head in a perfect circle, then veered away again, and a shining green feather floated down into his lap.

'I suppose that means yes,' Tad said, feeling suddenly happy and very excited. 'I'll come then. I'll really like that. But can you let me out of here now? I want to explore!'

He'd half expected the cliff in front of him to open itself up and let him through, or for a staircase to miraculously appear up the rock wall. Instead he heard a voice calling down to him from above.

'Tad! Are you there? Where are you? Tad!'

'Matthew!' yelled Tad joyfully. 'I'm down here! It's great here but I'm stuck. I can't get out.'

There was a long moment of silence while Matthew looked down at him, and Tad's heart stood still. He'd never been at anyone's mercy before. It felt really scary.

If Matthew walks away, I'll be stuck here forever, he

thought, his knees feeling suddenly weak.

'Matthew?' he said, trying not to let his voice tremble. 'You won't – I mean, you wouldn't –'

'Shut up, Tad,' Matthew called down to him. 'I'm thinking.'

His head disappeared. Tad screwed his eyes up tight, crossed his fingers till they hurt and hoped with all his might.

'Listen, Tad,' Matthew's voice came again. 'I've found this long kind of vine thing. Like in Tarzan. It's really strong. I've tied one end to a tree up here and I'll chuck the other end down to you. You climb and I'll pull, OK?'

'OK,' said Tad, with a nervous gulp.

He grabbed hold of the swinging vine and began to try to climb it. It was easier than he'd thought. The vine seemed to carry him up, almost of its own accord. He scrambled over the lip of the precipice and found Matthew, scarlet in the face and sweating, lying in a heap on the ground.

'I've never pulled so hard in my life,' panted Matthew. 'My arms have come half out.'

'That was you, pulling me out?' said Tad, amazed. 'Um – thanks.'

He'd never said thank you to anyone before. It was easier than he'd thought.

He sat down on the ground beside Matthew and they looked at each other.

'You know what?' said Tad. 'I'm not going to bother with the holiday complex and the rollercoaster and the cable car and stuff.'

Matthew stared at him suspiciously.

'What are you going to do instead?'

'Nothing.'

'Nothing?'

'Nothing. I'm going to leave it all just like it is.'

A smile broke out on Matthew's face.

'No cages for the monkeys?'

'Na. Course not.'

'No computer games parks? No roller rinks? No cable cars?'

'Nope.'

'Just like it is?'

'Yep.'

'So what *are* you going to do then?'

'Well,' said Tad, drawing a deep breath. 'I thought that we, I mean you and me, if you like, we could sort of play, you know? Come here sometimes and just get to know everywhere, and camp out maybe, and swim in the sea, and climb the trees and watch the monkeys. Just – well – *be* here.'

A grin was splitting Matthew's face in half.

'You know what, Tad, that's a great idea. I'm glad your granddad gave you this mountain. I'm really glad it's yours.'

'Yeah, but it isn't. Not really,' said Tad, shaking his

head. 'It belongs to itself. It sort of told me that, down there. Come on, Matt. Let's go and explore!'

The Goddess and the Snake

A story from Ancient Greece

At the beginning of time, the great goddess rose up out of chaos, and danced alone on the water. A wind blew up behind her, and its breath was the wind of creation.

The goddess turned and caught the wind in her hands and it became the great snake, Ophion. She danced more and more wildly, and the snake twined himself around her. They became as one.

The goddess turned herself into a dove and flew low over the water. Then, when her time came, she laid an egg. Ophion coiled himself around it seven times and when at last it hatched, all creation spilled out of it; the sun, moon and stars, the hills and mountains, the rivers and lakes, the trees and plants and all living creatures.

The goddess and the snake made their dwelling on Mount Olympus. For a time, all was well, but the snake, growing proud, claimed to be the creator of all things, and the goddess, in her fury, banished him forever to the darkness of the Underworld.

Black Mamba

'Is that him then? Is that my uncle?'

'Yes.'

Jonas squinted into the strong African sunlight towards the gap in the thorn fence which made the entrance to his father's compound. His mother had been squatting by a tray full of lentils, picking them over, but now she stood up, shook out her full skirt and crossed the bare ground towards the gate. Jonas followed.

His Uncle Nathan was smart. A real town guy. He wore a blue suit and a wide patterned tie. His hat had a white band round the crown. His belt had a big metal buckle.

Uncle Nathan had turned and was looking up the lane, waiting for Aaron, Jonas's father, who was driving the family's three cows home from their evening drink at the river.

'Hey brother! How are you?'

'Fine, just fine. How are you yourself?'

The two men slapped hands in the air, then embraced. The cows pushed past them to their pen inside the fence. Uncle Nathan backed away, putting up his hands as if he was nervous of the animals' long horns.

Aaron laughed.

'Look at you! Forgotten what it's like out here already. That one, Brown Ear, you used to ride on her back when you were a kid.'

Uncle Nathan wrinkled his nose and lifted his foot to inspect the sole of his shoe. He was standing near the old-fashioned round thatched hut where Jonas's mother stored the crop of maize cobs. The brim of his hat caught on the low thatched eaves. It toppled off his head into the dust. He picked it up and dusted it fastidiously. He looked as out of place in this little rural farm as a peacock on a dung heap.

Jonas's mother stepped forward.

'Welcome, brother,' she said shyly, holding out her hand. He shook it.

'You haven't changed, Charity. Pretty as ever. And this is Jonas. No more kids, Aaron? Why ever? You don't know your duty to your wife?'

He dug Aaron in the ribs. Aaron smiled uneasily. Charity stiffened with embarrassment, and Jonas looked swiftly at his father, then away again. It didn't do, in this family, to mention that there'd been no more children after him. It cut too deep for jokes.

Later, after supper, Nathan tipped back his chair and said, 'What is there, then, down here? Is it all still as dead as ever? Where does a man go in the evening?'

'He stays at home with his family,' Charity said softly, then laughed to show that she didn't mean to cause offence.

Uncle Nathan raised his eyebrows.

'What kind of a man are you, Aaron? You stay at home, tied to your wife's apron strings?'

'I go out sometimes,' Aaron said awkwardly. 'When I feel like it. A new bar's opened in the village since you left.'

'Then what are we waiting for?' Uncle Nathan said, and stood up.

They came home late. Jonas had been asleep, but he heard them stumble in. He also heard his mother's raised voice, sharp and anxious, from the other room, and a few grunts from his father. Then Uncle Nathan came in and flopped down heavily on the bed beside Jonas. He began to snore at once.

Jonas woke early. Grey dawn light was seeping through the shutters. His uncle had rolled over, taking the blanket with him, but it wasn't just the cold that had pulled Jonas out of sleep. There had been a noise.

It came again, from somewhere overhead. A sliding, dragging noise.

Rats in the roof, Jonas thought doubtfully.

His mother was up now. He could hear the creak as she

opened the wooden shutters, and then came the hiss of gas as she lit the jet under the kettle.

Jonas forgot the strange noise above, got up and pulled on his clothes. He was ready for breakfast.

The big black mamba had lain up in the space between the corrugated iron roof and the plywood ceiling for the whole of the last month. She had been digesting a couple of large rats, and hadn't moved a muscle in all that time. Now, though, she was hungry again. What Jonas had heard was the shuffle as she unravelled herself from the comfortable coil in which she had been lying.

While Jonas was eating his breakfast, the snake above the ceiling glided across to a place where the corner of one of the roof's iron sheets had worked loose and shifted sideways, leaving a small gap. She pushed her head out through it and looked down. There were some likely-looking holes running under the wall of the house, where rats might be lurking. Her slender forked tongue flickered in and out, testing the air for scents, but the mixture of cooking smells and human odours confused her. It was impossible to pick up anything useful. She would wait until the roof space had warmed up properly. Then her sluggish blood would be quickened. She would glide down the trunk of the papaya tree that grew so conveniently beside the house, and begin her hunt.

Jonas didn't see the snake until late that afternoon. He had, as usual, walked the five miles home from school and he was hot and tired, looking forward to a long cool drink of water and a mango from the huge glossy-leafed tree that overhung the cattle pen.

The mamba was halfway up the papaya stem, climbing fast, when Jonas spotted her. He stood, quite unable to move, just watching, as the snake's head reached delicately across the space separating the tree from the house, then disappeared under the eaves. The whole long length of her, three metres at least Jonas reckoned, slid out of sight as smoothly as a trickle of water slipping down a drain.

Afterwards he could never explain, either to himself or to anyone else, why he hadn't said anything about the mamba.

Perhaps it was because he hadn't quite believed his eyes. The snake had moved so calmly, with such confidence, as if it was simply going home after a day's business away, as naturally as Jonas, coming home after school. Or perhaps he'd known what would happen if he ran into the house, shouting out that a huge black mamba was up in the roof space. There would have been a mad panic, a fearsome fuss. Sticks would have been poked in to force the snake out. Then it would have been beaten to a pulp in a passion of fear and loathing.

Jonas knew as soon as he saw it, that he didn't want the snake to die. He wasn't being brave. The mamba sent shivers of fear all the way down his spine. It was more that the creature was – well, beautiful and private. Interesting, too. No, more than that. Fascinating.

In any case, he didn't have a chance to say anything. While he was standing stock still, his uncle came up behind him and slapped him on the shoulder.

'What did they teach you in school today then? How to work hard and be a good boy?'

Charity appeared at the door of the house.

'There you are, Jonas,' she said sharply. 'Come inside and start your homework.'

The secret of the snake lay heavily inside Jonas over the next few days. He watched out for it as best he could, hoping to see it again. Every morning when he went out, and in the afternoon when he came home, he looked up at the hole, which he could just make out in the shadowy eaves. In the evening, as he did his homework or went around the compound doing chores for his mother, he kept the slim trunk of the papaya tree in view as much as he could.

He only saw the snake once. He caught a glimpse of the last half metre of tail disappearing into the roof space on the second day. He was pleased, but guilty; pleased because he'd wondered if he had only imagined it after all, and guilty in case it came down and bit someone to death while he was out.

After that, he saw and heard nothing for a week.

The mamba was still there though. She had caught another small rat on the second day and had gone home to the roof space to digest it. Once satisfied, she didn't need or want to move again, but lay quite still for the whole seven days in a digestive stupor.

But somewhere, in the back of her quiet, torpid mind, a need was making her uneasy. She had grown again recently, and her old skin was uncomfortably tight. She was beginning to feel the urge to loosen it, to scrape it off and wriggle free.

The week had passed slowly and uncomfortably for Jonas. His mother was short-tempered with him, and all but silent in front of the men. His father had taken to going out every night and was brusque and red-eyed in the morning. Only Uncle Nathan was the same all the time, hearty and vain.

The black mamba began working herself out of her skin on Sunday evening, when for once Aaron and Uncle Nathan had stayed at home.

'I keep telling you, Aaron,' Uncle Nathan was saying, as they sat eating the rich chicken stew that Charity had prepared, 'you'd be much better off in the city. I could get you a good job, I'm sure.'

'How could you do that? I thought you'd lost your own job,' Charity said with careful politeness.

Uncle Nathan waved his arms.

'Contacts, Charity. Opportunities abound for the smart man. Look at you, Aaron. You want to be a country mouse all your life?'

Jonas wasn't listening. He'd heard a sound overhead. More than a sound. A long slow undertone of shifting and scraping.

What's it doing up there? he thought.

Surreptitiously, he looked up and scanned the ceiling in case there were any holes he'd never noticed before. What if the snake's head was to poke down suddenly? What if it dropped right down into the room on top of them?

He felt hot, then cold, and wiped his sweating forehead with the back of his sleeve.

'I've got our father's land to look after, Nathan, in case you've forgotten,' Aaron was saying.

Uncle Nathan laughed.

'This farm? But you have a strong healthy wife! And your great big son! How many people do you need to run a little place like this?'

There was a thump overhead. Jonas imagined a coil of the snake falling on to the boards as it writhed about up there. His eyes flew to each of the others in turn, but no one else had heard.

Aaron and Nathan went outside the house after supper. They sat on a pair of stools in the warm night air, under the blaze of diamond stars that studded the black velvet sky. Nathan was peeling and slicing mangoes from the old tree, and handing them to his brother to eat.

'It's not as if she's given you any more children,' Jonas heard his uncle say quietly. 'What kind of a man has only one son? If you come with me, you can get yourself a new young wife.'

Charity slammed the shutters to and moved the kerosene lamp to her side of the table.

'If you want to read you'll have to do it round this side,' she snapped. 'I need the light to sew.'

She looked so forbidding that Jonas didn't dare say anything about the snake, or about anything else.

He stood up.

'I'm going to bed, Mama,' he said.

In the next room, he lit the candle by the bed, then held it up high so that its beams lit every corner of the ceiling. He'd never seen a hole up there, but it was as well to make sure. He checked that the shutters were closed tight, looked under the furniture and in every corner, then hopped into bed and tucked his mosquito net in all the way round.

Jonas was used to the regular quiet sounds of the homestead in the evening, to his parents' murmured voices and occasional yawns, to the click of the latch as his father went out to check on the cows, and the splash as his mother threw the water from her washing bowl out into the yard.

It was different tonight. The adults' voices were tight with tension, and every now and then one was raised in anger.

'What do you mean, woman, that I'd never get a job in the city? Look at Nathan. Hasn't he done all right for himself?'

Jonas didn't want to listen. He covered his head with the blanket, but he could hear his father's voice just the same.

'Nathan's right. If we sold the cows you and Jonas could manage this place on your own. And I'd send money home to you. Of course I would.'

Charity spoke quietly and Jonas couldn't hear what she was saying, but he could tell that she was anxious. Her voice was gentle but firm, and shot through with scorn. Every now and then he could hear Uncle Nathan interrupting her impatiently, but once he'd finished talking, she would start up again, persistent and unstoppable. His father said nothing.

Jonas tossed about in bed that night and woke heavy-eyed the next morning. Uncle Nathan was still asleep, but outside Jonas could hear the sound of hammering. He dressed quickly. He was cutting it fine if he didn't want to be late for school.

'What's Father doing?' he asked Charity as he quickly ate his porridge.

'Mending the post in the cattle pen,' she said. 'He's decided to get on with repairs round the house today.'

He couldn't tell, from the tone of her voice, what she was thinking.

As he stepped outside he wrinkled his nose at a faint unaccustomed smell, something dry and powdery, with a tang of spice to it. He thought no more of it and set off at a smart trot on the five-mile run to school.

By the time the snake felt warm enough to move easily, the house and yard were deserted. Charity was hoeing the maize patch. Aaron was out cutting branches to patch the fence. Uncle Nathan had gone off whistling into the village.

The smell of curry powder, which the mamba had released when she'd shed her skin, clung to her still as she spiralled down the papaya tree and slipped across the open space in front of the house to a patch of shadow under the water tank, where several promising holes suggested the presence of rats. She coiled herself out of sight and settled down, as still as a stone carving, to watch and wait.

Aaron didn't see her, though he walked past within two metres of her, on his way to mend the roof of the house. Charity came even closer, no more than a couple of feet away, as she drew water off at the tap for her chickens. The snake eyed her long full skirt nervously, but sensing no threat, she kept still.

The family of rats who lived down the hole smelled the mamba's new skin. It alarmed them enough to keep them in their burrow all day. By mid-afternoon, however, they'd become used to it, and as everything else seemed to be quiet and safe, the boldest of them stuck his head out of the hole, looked round, saw nothing and stepped out into the open.

The mamba had waited for this moment, with infinite patience, through the heat of the day. She gathered herself and struck with the speed of a bullet, inflicting four bites in as many seconds. An instant later, the rat was dead, succumbing to the deadly poison, and the mamba swallowed it slowly, her throat rippling as

35

the small body began its long journey to her stomach.

The snake had been so swift and silent that the rat had barely had time to squeak, and after another ten minutes another rat came out. It went the way of the first.

It was late afternoon now, and the sun was beginning its slow fall to the horizon. Soon the temperature would start to drop. The snake needed to be safely home before the chill of the evening thickened her blood and slowed her down.

She was about to set off, back to the papaya tree and the gap under the eaves, when Charity came towards the water tank. The snake lay, her watching eyes on the bare brown leg, but once again she sensed no threat and didn't move.

Charity filled a pot and went back towards the house, slopping a few drops out on to the ground as she went. She set the pot down on the floor inside the door and went off to collect her washing, which had been drying some way away, on the bushes by the stream.

A few minutes later, Jonas sprinted into the compound, tired after his long run home from school and breathless from the last dash up the hill. He ran into the house, dipped a tumbler into the pot of cool water and drank it down, then threw himself on to a chair by the table, yawned, and dropped his head down onto his arms.

The mamba had become aware that she was thirsty. She flicked her forked tongue over the damp patch in the hard-baked earth below the tap of the water tank. A line of drips led away from it towards the open door of the house. Moving fast, the snake followed the trail, and seconds later she was exploring the threshold with her tongue. She found the pot almost at once and lifting her slate grey head over it, put down her mouth and began to drink. She finished drinking, raised her head from the pot, coiled herself in a patch of warm sunlight inside the door and stopped moving.

Some noise, perhaps the faint rasp of her scales against the earthen side of the pot, had brought Jonas out of his doze. He lifted his head, and saw the mamba lying between him and the doorway.

For a few moments, his mind was as frozen as his body. He felt nothing but terror. But then his fear began to change into a kind of exhilaration. The snake lay comfortably, seemingly unafraid, as if she had a right to be in the house, as if it belonged to her.

Jonas studied her admiringly, marvelling at the purple bloom on the grey scales along her spine, shading to ivory where they disappeared under her belly. He wanted to approach her, even to put out his hand and touch her satin back.

Are you crazy? he heard himself think.

He had been staring at the snake for a long time, trying to think out what he should do, when he became aware of voices in the distance. Uncle Nathan was back, talking loudly to someone, his mother he supposed, halfway down the lane.

They'll see you, Jonas silently told the snake. They'll get you. Or they won't see you, and they'll tread on you, and you'll kill them. I've got to get you out of here.

The mamba moved her head as if she had heard him, swivelling it slowly towards the door. For a moment Jonas thought she was leaving of her own accord. Then he realised that she had merely been watching a beetle, which had walked obliviously past her nose, and had then veered off and wandered away along the wall.

An idea came to Jonas. Cautiously, taking care not to move too suddenly, he put his hand up to the box on the shelf above the table, where Charity kept her money, and lifted it down. As quietly as he could, he eased off the lid and picked out a coin. Then, bending down, he balanced the coin on its rim and, with a wordless prayer, rolled it towards the snake.

The coin seemed to move with unnatural slowness and for a long, heart-stopping moment Jonas thought it would hit one of the steely coils and rouse the snake to anger. But it didn't even reach her. It stopped rolling, wobbled, then tipped over and settled with a final clatter a few centimetres from the snake's tail.

Jonas took a deep breath, fumbled for a second coin and tried again. This one was luckier. It rolled right past the mamba's nose, and on out of the door. The mamba, her interest aroused, lifted her head and watched it go.

His confidence growing, Jonas tried again. The third coin went wide. The fourth trundled steadily past the snake and even stayed upright when it bounced down from the threshold, travelling on undaunted for another two metres out into the yard.

Curiosity overcame the mamba. In one quick fluid motion she had slipped out through the doorway after it. She flickered her tongue across its metallic surface but it held no interest for her. She turned away towards the papaya tree, ready to go home.

At that very moment, Uncle Nathan, with Charity behind him, came into the yard.

Uncle Nathan saw the mamba first, let out a roar of terror and dived behind Charity. She took no notice of him. After one horrified glance at the snake, she had looked over at Jonas, who was now standing in the doorway of the house.

'Don't move, child,' she called out.

Aaron appeared. He took in the situation at once, crossed to the cattle pen and began to tug at one of the stakes that formed the fence.

'Wait,' he said quietly. 'I'll deal with it. Just keep still all of you.'

Uncle Nathan took no notice. He was edging surreptitiously sideways, obviously intent on getting behind the house, so that solid walls would be between himself and the snake. He was moving jerkily, stopping and starting. He had halted now right in front of the papaya tree, and without realising it, had blocked the mamba's way home.

Replete with rat, unaware that the large cumbersome creatures who had appeared in the yard might be a danger to her, the mamba had been gliding quietly towards her papaya tree. The man standing in front of it irritated her. She flattened her neck to make a hood, lifted her head and hissed.

'Keep still, Nathan,' Charity called out in a hoarse whisper. 'Don't aggravate it.'

Behind her, Aaron was still wrestling with the fence, trying to wrench out the stake that he'd tied in place that morning.

Uncle Nathan had frozen. His mouth had fallen open and his eyes were wide with horror. The mamba, wanting to force him out of her way, opened her jaws in a threatening gape. When he still didn't move, she reared up, balancing her lithe muscular body on her long tail. She was standing formidably high now, her head on a level with Uncle Nathan's neck.

As if an electrical current had passed through him, Uncle Nathan came to life. With a wail, he turned and raced past Charity and Aaron, rushed out of the compound, and disappeared down the lane.

The snake, seeing her way clear, shot up the tree and stretched out her neck towards the familiar hole under the eaves. It wasn't there. She poked her head backwards and forwards, searching for it, but Aaron had done his repairs too thoroughly. There was no way in for her now.

There was a commotion in the yard below her. Aaron had freed the stick from the fence and was trying to get to the tree to attack the snake, but Charity and Jonas had wrapped their arms round him, and were hanging on to him with all their strength.

'What are you doing?' Aaron was shouting furiously. 'Get away from me! I'm going to kill it!'

'No, Father,' panted Jonas.

'Aaron, let it go,' pleaded Charity. 'It'll bite you! It'll attack you! Come away!'

The mamba, alarmed, scanned one last time along the eaves, but seeing no way in she gave up. She doubled back along her own length, raced down from the tree, shot across the dusty compound, in one long streak of grey, and disappeared through the fence.

Aaron shook off his wife and son and glared at them.

'Are you mad, both of you? I'd have killed it for sure if it wasn't for you.'

But Jonas had felt his father's arm trembling, and sensed that he was secretly relieved.

Charity was staring at her husband with admiration.

'Eh, Aaron, you are a man,' she said. 'That snake, it must have enough poison in it to lay out a whole army.'

'Uncle Nathan thought so, anyway. Did you see how fast he ran?' said Jonas, and he and his mother burst out laughing.

Slowly, the anger drained out of Aaron's face, and a moment later the three of them stood together, rocking backwards and forwards, shaking with paroxysms of laughter.

Something had changed, Jonas could sense it. The cloud that had hung over the house since his uncle had come had blown away.

The mamba, streaking out of the compound, had only one need in her mind. She had to find somewhere to rest before night fell. She slowed down once she felt safe and began to explore purposefully. She was looking for an old termite nest perhaps, or a deserted burrow, or a hole in a hollow tree.

She found it just as the huge red ball of the sun touched the far horizon. Villagers had tied cylinders of wood and matting up in a tall baobab tree, hoping to entice bees to make their hives in them. The mamba investigated them one by one. Only two were occupied. She chose an empty one near the top of the tree, which was wedged firmly between two stout branches. It would easily take her weight. She glided into it, arranged her coils, and sank down into the contented torpor of digestion.

Jonas never saw the mamba again. He looked out for her for a while, but slowly she slipped from his memory. It was a long time, too, before he saw his uncle again. Nathan had disappeared back to the city the day after his encounter with the mamba, taking his tie and his banded hat and his shiny belt buckle with him.

There had been no more talk of Aaron joining him.

Nothing, now, would have dragged him away from his wife who, as if by a miracle, twelve years after giving birth to Jonas, was expecting his second child.

The Flood

The Book of Genesis

God saw that man was filled with violence and thought only of evil things. He was grieved, and his heart was filled with pain. He said, 'I will destroy all the creatures which I have made: men and women, the beasts, the creeping things and the birds of the air, for they are very wicked.'

Now of all the people on the earth, only Noah found favour in God's eyes, for he was a good man.

God said to Noah, 'You must make an ark out of cypress wood and make rooms inside it and cover it with tar both inside and out so that it is waterproof. The ark must be 133 metres long and 22 metres wide and 13 metres high. Make a roof over it with a window and put a door in the side. Make three decks inside the ark, a top, a middle and a lower deck.

'I am going to bring a great flood over all the earth, and everything that lives will die. But you and your wife and your sons and your sons' wives will go into the ark, and you will take with you two of every kind of animal, a male and a female, to keep them alive. You will also take with you all the food you need, both for your family and for the animals.'

So Noah made the ark as God had told him.

After seven days, a great flood came upon the earth. Fountains of water from deep underground burst out, and the floodgates of heaven opened. On that very day, Noah went into the ark with his wife, his sons, Shem, Ham and Japheth, and their wives, and every kind of bird and animal and creeping thing. They went into the ark two by two as God had commanded. And the Lord shut them in.

For forty days and forty nights the flood grew greater and greater and it lifted the ark off the ground. Still the flood went on rising until it covered every hill and mountain. All the people and creatures of the earth were drowned. Only Noah remained alive and those that were with him in the ark.

At last God shut the fountains of the deep, and closed the floodgates of heaven, and the waters began to go down. The bottom of the ark came to rest on the mountains of Ararat, and the tops of the mountains could be seen.

Noah opened the window and sent out a dove. She found nowhere to land, so she returned to the ark, and Noah put out his hand and brought her back in.

Seven days later, he sent her out again. In the evening, when she returned, she held an olive leaf in her beak. So Noah knew that the waters had gone down.

Seven more days he waited, then he sent the dove out again. This time she flew away and did not return. Now Noah knew that the ground was dry.

Noah and his family and all the living creatures came out of the ark. Then Noah built an altar to the Lord, and offered him burnt offerings.

God smelled the sweet smell of Noah's sacrifice, and he said in his heart, 'I will never again curse the ground, because of human wickedness.

> *While the earth remaineth,*
> *seed time and harvest, and cold and heat,*
> *and summer and winter, and day and night,*
> *shall not cease.'*

God blessed Noah and his sons, and he said to them, 'Be fruitful and multiply, and fill the earth with your children. All the animals and birds, every creature that moves on the earth and all the fish of the sea, will fear you, and are given into your hands, and all living things may be your food.'

And God gave a promise to Noah saying, 'Never again shall a flood destroy the life of the earth. I set my rainbow in the sky as a sign of the covenant between me and all living creatures. When I see it, I shall remember the promise I have made.'

Long Wing

The huge wave crashed against the jagged black rocks and a plume of spray rose high into the air. A sudden sharp squall picked it up and hurled its tiny droplets of water and salt on to the tough tussocky grass that grew on the slopes high above.

Sky King, sitting on his rough nest of twigs and moss, had been half asleep, but the spray woke him and turning his head he scanned the long grey expanse of sea. His mate had been gone for more than a week and hunger was making him uneasy.

He shifted his body, but he moved too quickly and the precious egg, that for days past had been slowly splitting open under the weak assaults from the chick struggling inside, threatened to roll out of the nest. Gently, Sky King prodded it back into place, settled himself again and resumed his long wait.

And then he felt a feeble fluttering, as something moved under him. The chick, his chick, was hatching. Carefully, he stepped aside. The baby albatross's hooked bill had finally cut a long breach in the confining case of shell, and the stubby rudiments of two wings, covered in wet down, were free at last. Weak from the effort, dazzled by the light and smells and sounds of the world, the baby staggered out, and took his first stumbling step.

Sky King had been so intent on the birth of his son that he had not seen Silver, his mate, approach, but she was suddenly beside him, bending her great white neck, nuzzling the baby with her long hooked bill. Gently she forced up his head. The chick opened his beak and she squirted a stream of rich warm oil from her stomach into his.

Sky King could wait no longer. He had to get back to sea and feed before hunger made him weak. He waddled on his great grey webbed feet, speckled with unusual stains of brown, to the top of the grassy slope and spread out his huge wings. He began to run downhill and the wind caught him and lifted him into flight. He circled the headland once, looking down on his mate and his newly hatched son, then he turned away and soared off over the great Southern Ocean.

The autumn and winter had passed for Long Wing in endless days of waiting for his parents to come winging home to the nest with food for his ravenous stomach.

At first, either Sky King or Silver had stayed with him all the time. They had sheltered him under their soft warm breasts from the fierce spring blizzards that sometimes whipped across the headland, and had seen off, with furious squawks and flappings of their giant wings, the rapacious skuas, who came with sharp beaks and vicious claws to tear and devour any unprotected chicks.

But as the months had passed and Long Wing had grown, his parents, needing to find ever greater quantities of food for his huge appetite, had left him for longer and longer intervals.

The winter had been long and terrible. Stinging flakes of snow had swept continously over the bare headland, driven on violent winds from the chill Antarctic wastes, from whose shore ice had spread out in great white sheets across the freezing sea. Alone on his nest, Long Wing had sat and waited to be fed. Hunkered down in his fluff through the endless nights, he spent the short days gazing out to sea, watching for his father or mother's return.

In that time, he had moved through many transformations, growing first into a vast ball of downy fluff, then slowly putting forth feathers, and long slim wings, developing a powerful beak on which ribbed nostrils lay like delicate flutes along each side.

It had been many days now since his parents had visited him. Silver had flown away weeks earlier, and since then Long Wing had seen Sky King only once. He had landed reluctantly, his gorge only half full, and had needed much persuasion, much tapping on the bill and many shrill cries, before he would regurgitate his food for the rapacious chick.

Long Wing was hungry, and another sensation, a kind of curiosity, was growing inside him too. He watched, head tilted on one side, as another albatross from a nearby nest side ran expertly down the slope, its wings outstretched, and soared away into the wind.

He had been batting his wings for weeks in practice, and he was beginning to trust in their strength. Raising them experimentally, and hesitating frequently to look about him, Long Wing waddled slowly to the edge of the cliff. He stood there for a long time as if screwing up his courage, then he held his untried wings invitingly up to the wind. A squall caught him. He was lifted off his feet for a moment, but the wind suddenly dropped again. He would have plunged helplessly down the sheer cliff to his death on the sharp mussel-covered rocks below, if a last little gust hadn't caught him and blown him back on to the grass.

He had not felt any fear. The short sensation of being airborne had been good. The lull had only lasted a moment or two. He could feel the wind again now, ruffling his feathers, and it excited him. More boldly, he spread his wings out again and took a couple of lolloping strides towards the edge of the cliff. This time the wind picked him up securely in its friendly grasp and he felt, for the first time, its rushing power as he let it carry him up and away.

He tried to copy the older birds as they circled round the headland, using their motionless wings as sails, picking up every nuance of the turbulent flow of air, but he was too clumsy, too untried. He found himself swooping down, closer and closer to the sea.

He had not realised, from his eyrie up on the cliff, that the sea moved so strangely. The cold green landscape rocked up and down, making the waves of the air above it, on which his wings were relying, falter and ripple in unfamiliar, unpredictable ways. He was so low now that one webbed foot dipped into the sea. He flapped his wings twice, trying to pull himself up, but the air currents were against him. He gave into the inevitable and sank down on to the water.

It was a new sensation, floating on the shifting transparent surface, his feet piercing through it as he learned to ride the waves. He sat on the water and looked about, getting used to the moving walls of grey green swell, the patterns of white foam on their gleaming sides and the endlessly changing horizon.

Then something caught his eye. A pale shape, round at one end with short streamer-like projections at the other, flickered through the water, almost under his bill. He plunged at it curiously, and the hooked end of his bill touched it. The thing jerked away and shimmered down into the dark depths. But Long Wing had caught a taste of it. It was a squid, his favourite food. Excited, and urgent with hunger, he paddled himself forwards, his eyes on the water, looking for another one.

He was surprised by a sudden noise behind him. A shag shot out of the water at speed, running on tiptoe across the waves to take off, shrieking a piercing cry of danger. Though it made Long Wing uneasy, he did not understand where the danger might come from. He stayed sitting, confused. He did not see the long fin that was speeding towards him, breaking through the surface of the wave.

The shark rose up under him, jaws agape, and it would have caught him if a lucky buffet from the turbulent wind had not suddenly knocked him out of range of the rows of sharp teeth. Terrified, Long Wing twisted and turned, struggling to take off, but he had no idea how to lift himself up into the air. The shark whipped round and was on him again. Long Wing was in its mouth now. Its jaws were closing on his body.

Long Wing twisted his neck frantically from side to side. The only moving thing in the smooth grey surface of the shark's head was its small round eye. Desperately, he jabbed at it with the full force of his bill. The shark's grip faltered. It dived, trying to take Long Wing with it, to drown him in the depths, where it could eat him in peace. But Long Wing pecked furiously again at the rolling eye.

The shark, moving more slowly this time, made one last effort. It wheeled round in the water to come up behind Long Wing. The young albatross's every sense was now alive with terror and rage and he turned and raised his huge wings, lowering his bill, ready for the fight.

The shark had had enough. It sped away through the water, its fin hidden almost at once by a wave. Long Wing had had enough too. He held his wings up to the wind, as if he was begging it to lift him into the friendlier sky, but he was in a trough now between two waves and the air was still. He raised himself out of the water and began to paddle, then run, frantically over the surface, wings outstretched. The water trough beneath him was rising now into the crest of the next wave. As it rose to the top, a gust of wind picked him up and carried him into its welcoming currents.

The summer was good to Long Wing. Soaring alone on huge outstretched wings round the great southern oceans of the world, travelling sometimes hundreds of miles in a single day, he learned to know every trick of the wind, to use every gust, every flutter of turbulence. In the violent storms that turned the sea into shifting mountain ranges of water, he would swoop down the long trough between two waves, eyes alert for the pale flash of a dead squid floating on the surface, or a rolling swarm of prawn-like krill. He would follow whales, ready to snap up any titbits that floated out of their vast jaws. He flew low over icebergs that lumbered through the sea like huge sculptures, shot through with blue and green light, their sides scoured and carved by the salt waves that smacked endlessly against their frozen sides.

Sometimes he saw other albatrosses. He joined them occasionally as they squabbled round the offal flung from the deck of a fishing boat. Once, as he circled round a trawler, waiting for the magical supply of food to appear, he met his father.

They had landed together on the water and thrust out their necks, their bills wide open, calling to each other with loud croaking cries. And then the food had showered down on them from the deck above and they had joined the other snapping, voracious birds at the feast.

He never saw his mother.

More than two years had passed since Long Wing had flown the nest. He had survived his third winter at sea and was ready for another spring. He was a powerful bird now, still immature but experienced, a skilful fisher, a brilliant navigator of the wind.

While Long Wing soared aloft, his eyes ever scanning the water for the gleam of a squid or the flash of a fish, 10,000 miles to the north two men were working on the covered deck of a big ship.

They were too used to the stench of fish, that had penetrated every corner of the vessel, to be properly nauseated but they turned their faces into the breeze, whenever they had the chance to breathe gusts of cleaner air.

'You've signed up for the whole season?'

The man with the mole on his cheek straightened his back and stood up. His companion, still bending over the oily mechanism on the ship's vast empty deck, looked up at him.

'Sure. You mean you haven't?'

Mole Cheek shrugged, watching with interest as the other man deftly manoeuvred the mechanism's complex parts with his eight remaining fingers.

'Yeah,' he said. 'I've signed. The money's good.'

'You're not married then?'

Mole Cheek screwed a roll of saliva up on his tongue and spat it out over the side of the ship.

'What if I am? She gets the money. Some of it. What else does she want?'

Eight Fingers said nothing. He turned the last nut with his spanner and stood up. Mole Cheek watched curiously as he wiped his oily fingers on a cloth.

'How did you lose them, anyway?'

'What? These?' Eight Fingers held up his right hand. The first and second fingers had been sliced off at the lowest joint. Only a couple of short stumps remained. 'Caught them in the winch last season. Bringing in a catch of tuna. Biggest I ever saw and I've seen some. Took my eye off what I was doing for a couple of seconds and a hook whipped round . . .'

'OK.' Mole Cheek had looked away. 'I get the picture.'

'Funny thing was,' Eight Fingers said, 'it was all the

fault of a damned bird. We were bringing the line in, full of tuna, and there was this dead bird, a silver coloured thing, caught on one of the hooks. Another one, a great feathered monster with ugly dirty patches on its feet, flew right down to it. It kept pecking at the man who was getting the dead one off the hook. The others tried to beat it off but it wouldn't go. I was so busy laughing at them all, slipping around in all the tuna blood, slapping away at this crazy bird that I took my eyes off the job and the next thing I knew . . .'

'Yeah,' said Mole Cheek quickly. 'What kind of bird did you say it was?'

'Albatross. It was weird, you know . . .'

'What? What was weird?'

Eight Fingers put down his rag and began to walk across the clanging metal deck towards the companionway.

'It was almost as if the thing was – oh, I don't know – demented. With rage or grief or something.'

'Maybe the dead one was its mate or something.'

'Its mate? Don't be soft. It was a bird, not some fancy Romeo.'

As the fleets of trawlers from the fish-hungry nations of the north began their long journey towards the tuna-killing fields of the southern ocean, spring approached.

Long Wing was restless. All through the winter he had flown and hunted alone, meeting other birds only when he raced them to snatch the best morsels that fell from the occasional trawler into the sea. But now he was aware of his own kind as never before.

On a day when a sharp spring breeze was blowing and the sunlight splintered on the rippling water, it was calmer than it had been for months. He watched as a young female flew below him, her black tipped wings dazzling white against the blue sea.

He dropped down to her altitude and followed her. She was circling round a group of six or eight other albatrosses who were bobbing about on the surface of the sea close together. They were gesticulating excitedly, although there was no shoal of fish that Long Wing could see, no boiling mass of krill.

The female ahead wheeled round and swooped down to land beside them. At once a young male bird paddled enthusiastically up to her. He stretched his head up as high as it would go, waggling it excitedly from side to side. She turned away, and he raised himself out of the water and stretched out his wings, curving them towards her and calling loudly.

For the first time in his life, Long Wing wanted the company of other birds. He dropped down on to the water beside the young female. He stretched his neck and called as he had seen the older birds do, and lifted his wings and beat them once or twice. The others, seeing the dark brown tips to his feathers and knowing he was only a juvenile who would not breed for years yet, ignored him and went on with their dancing display.

Long Wing stayed among the party of albatrosses all through the spring day, excited and content. They took off as evening came, some singly, some in pairs, leaving him alone on the water.

As luck would have it, a passing pair of sperm whale, who had gorged themselves on squid earlier that day, released dozens of them from their gaping mouths. The lifeless squid floated to the surface and Long Wing feasted that night as he had never done before.

The men had worked all day on the covered deck of the fishing vessel, spearing bait on to thousands of hooks. The baited lines lay in holding trays along the deck, ready to be paid out into the ocean. The men were hungry and thirsty. Their backs ached and their fingers were numb with cold. Above all, their tempers were foul.

'Frozen!' said Eight Fingers in disgust, tipping a box full of rock hard fish on to the deck.

'So what if it is?' growled Mole Cheek, picking up a piece of stiff flesh and ramming it on to a razor-sharp hook.

'So it won't sink, that's what,' spat Eight Fingers, 'so the lousy birds'll plunge for it, so we'll pull in a line of dead albatrosses tomorrow instead of tuna, so bang goes our bonus. That's what.'

Mole Cheek looked briefly at the narrow strip of sea and sky that was visible through the long opening in the stern of the covered deck. A flock of albatrosses flew low over the water, waiting for bounty to fall from the ship.

'And there they are, the stupid gits, lining up to get it.'

'My heart bleeds,' said Eight Fingers, holding up his mutilated hand. 'They owe me for this. Give me a gun and I'd shoot the lot of them.'

When darkness fell the lines began to pay out and the ship began to move slowly ahead through the water, leaving the murderous snaking trail of hooks, eighty miles long, in its wake.

By dawn the first part of the line of baited hooks had sunk down into the sea and from some of them huge, heavy tuna fish already hung, twitching in their death throes. But the fish on the last part of the line, nearest to the ship, were still partially frozen. They floated near the surface, deadly snares, and as the sky lightened, the flock of twenty or thirty albatrosses and shearwaters, who had spent the night close to the ship waiting for the food to appear, caught sight of them. They plunged down towards the baited hooks, still just a few feet below the surface of the water.

Long Wing had been flying all night, half sleeping on the wing, and it was well after dawn when he saw, far below, the big ship, chugging gently through the water. He made for it like an arrow, plunging down through the turbulent air to the place where a few birds were still squawking near the stern.

Only half the original flock were left. The others, the strongest ones, who had been able to fight off the smaller, weaker birds in the scramble for the bait, had already died, drowned, their bills caught in the deadly hooks.

But now the last section of line was sinking fast, pulled under by the weight of dead tuna and dead birds. Long Wing could see, disappearing tantalisingly out of sight, a morsel of fish that tempted him. He lowered his head, ready to dive for it, but he was too late. A shearwater, flying low overhead, had seen it too. It folded its wings and plunged like an arrow in front of Long Wing's eyes, caught the fish it its mouth, struggled desperately for a moment or two as the hook bit deeper into its throat, and died.

Long Wing took off into the wind. He circled a few times round the ship but the line had sunk now and there was no other sign that food would be forthcoming. Disappointed, he wheeled away and headed east, flying low over the water. Yesterday, 300 miles away to the east, he had found a rich source of krill. He would try his luck there again.

Long Wing was ten years old. He now wore the brilliant white feathers of adulthood and his powerful bill was a formidable fishing weapon. His magnificent black-tipped wings, that spanned three metres at full stretch, had mastered every subtle alteration of wind and air. His tireless strength could carry him for thousands of miles on his endless soaring flights as he circled and recircled the globe.

But now Long Wing had come in to land. He had flown home to the cliff top where he had fledged.

He had been at sea for so long that his first landing on the grassy headland had been clumsy. He might have crushed a leg if a lucky hummock of tussocky grass had not broken his fall.

He had chosen his nest site immediately. It had not been hard to find, a good, grassy spot, sheltered from the wind. He had had to drive away another questing male, but he had done this without much difficulty. His first effort at building had gone well. There were useful ferns and twigs and tussock grass lying all around.

It took Long Wing days to make his nest and it was far from finished when the first female arrived. Her mate, an older male on a nest site not far from Long Wing's, put up his wings and raucously called her in. She flew down beside him and they greeted each other with an ecstatic display of cries and gestures before they mated.

Long Wing watched the sky constantly, waiting for Wind Hover to appear. He had met her two years ago when, with other juveniles, he had returned to the headland to be with his kind, and he had courted her all through the long days of the previous summer. They had circled each other in slow dances. They had whistled and called and tapped their beaks. And they had flown together, diving and soaring, wheeling and plunging in perfect unison, as if they were two parts of the same creature. Only the autumn storms had driven them apart, to fish and fly alone through the long Antarctic winter.

All along the rocky headland, albatross pairs were busy, repairing nests, greeting each other, dancing out the rituals that bonded them. Long Wing walked restlessly round and round his nest, his eyes on the sky.

And then he saw her. She came in below the clouds, flying on the wind, her black eyes searching the crowded headland, looking for him. Long Wing lifted his head and called. For a moment Wing Hover seemed not to hear him. He called again, louder and more urgently. She wheeled round, looking for a place to land, and came down at last beside him.

For a moment or two they cried out loudly to each other, their heads raised, then Long Wing tugged gently at Wind Hover's wing feathers and she turned to face him, her bill slightly open, and they ducked and rolled their heads, softly touching each other. Wind Hover lifted her head to the sky, inviting Long Wing to groom her, and he dropped his bill into the soft mottled feathers on her neck, nibbling and stroking, perfectly content.

Later that day, they mated.

The large blotched egg had become the centre of Long Wing's life. Since Wind Hover had laid it, eleven weeks earlier, he had hardly seen her. As soon as she had come back to the nest from days of feeding out at sea, he had been driven by his own hunger to go in search of food.

She had never been gone for more than four days

before. He had seldom left her for more than three, though he had sometimes had to travel 500 miles in that time in search of food. Now, though, Wind Hover had been gone for nearly two weeks. Fretting with anxiety, Long Wing scanned the sky, calling to her, although he could see she was not there. He could not wait much longer. He had to feed soon.

Gingerly, he lifted himself up off his egg. For some days past, he had been excited by faint tappings and scratchings from inside the thick shell.

His movement seemed to rouse the chick. Long Wing heard a series of clicks and taps as its soft bill resumed the exhausting work of breaking through the shell. Gently, he laid his own bill against it, feeling the vibration of the struggling movements within.

He hesitated and looked up again into the sky. Where was Wind Hover? He lowered himself again on to his egg, protecting it with his great body from the keen spring wind that ripped across the headland. A moment later he was up again. His hunger was desperate now. He had to feed before he became too weak to fly.

He stepped awkwardly off his nest and fumbled at the egg with his beak. Every instinct was urging him to stay with it. Every pang of hunger was ordering him to go.

He lifted his head and gave one long, despairing cry, calling for Wind Hover, pleading for his chick. Then, without a backward glance, he spread his wings, ran down into the wind and soared away out to sea.

★ ★ ★

A thousand miles away, the rusting hulk of a fishing boat was steaming through the water, winching on board an endless line of twitching tuna fish.

'One for you!' Mole Cheek called out, unhooking a dead albatross and throwing its bedraggled body to the man beside him.

'Leave off, will you?' growled Eight Fingers, and picking up Wind Hover's body, he flung it out over the stern of the ship where it sank down into the sea.

Ninurta and Kur

An ancient story, 5,000 years old, from
Ur in Iraq

When all things were new, and Heaven and
Earth had only just been separated from each
other, the goddess Ereskigal was captured by
the snake-demon, Kur, who dragged her down to his dark
lair in the Underworld.

Ninurta, the god of thunder and of the earth's fertility,
had a magical weapon. This weapon spoke to him and
said, 'Ninurta, go down into the Underworld and rescue
the goddess Ereskigal.'

Ninurta listened to his weapon. He penetrated the evil
regions and found Kur, coiled snake-like in his den.
The god and the demon battled back and forth together,
but Kur the demon was too strong for Ninurta, and
Ninurta fled.

Once again, Ninurta's weapon spoke. 'Go back,' it
said, 'go down, and fight again.'

So Ninurta went down once more to the Underworld.
With new power, he attacked Kur. He struck him fiercely
with all his might, and at last he overcame him.

But while this fearsome war was being waged, disaster
had overcome the natural world. The primeval sea had
welled up from the deep places of the earth, flooding the

land and poisoning the fields with its salt. The plants had died, and the crops had withered on their stems.

The gods of the land begged the great Ninurta for his help. He heard them, and raised a vast pile of stones over the body of Kur, making a mountain to hold back the primeval sea. Now peace reigned, and the fresh waters of the Tigris flowed again, flushing away the salt and irrigating the fields. The plants grew and the crops ripened. Soon the war was forgotten, and Ninurta blessed the mountain he had made, and the sweet fruit that the earth brought forth.

Mr Hasbini's Garden

The boy was in the hospital office when the fighting started.

'Who are you looking for? What was his name again?' The clerk began to leaf without interest through a stack of files.

'Ramzi, I told you,' the boy said. 'He was at the secondary school. The one that was bombed. He's sixteen.'

'Didn't you come in here a few weeks ago?' the clerk said, looking up with a frown of irritation. 'I told you then that we'd had no boy of that name here.'

'But he might have been brought in later,' the boy said. 'Please. Please look.'

With no warning and with deafening force, a shell exploded nearby. The clerk disappeared under his desk as fast as a mouse bolting into a hole.

The boy darted to the door and out of the building. He

began to run, terrified of being inside in case the building collapsed around him.

The street was empty. Bicycles lay where people had thrown them down as they had dashed for cover. But the boy preferred to take the risk of being caught in the battle to the terror of being inside. He ran low to the ground, as fast as a hare, ducking and diving to make himself a harder target.

Shouts and explosions ahead made him swerve down a side alley. He ran fast, on and on, making for the edge of town.

At last he saw ahead the open road running through sun-baked fields and groves of orange trees. His pace slackened.

Safe, he thought, the word pounding in his head like the blood pounding through his heart. Safe, safe, safe here.

Then, on the road ahead, he became aware of a low, steady roar. The boy screwed his eyes up against the blinding sun. He could make out a group of tiny specks in the distance, growing infinitely slowly but with awful steadiness as they approached. The pulse-beat in his head changed.

Tanks, it went, tanks, tanks, tanks.

He looked round for a place to hide, and saw, a little way back from the road, a familiar pair of corrugated iron gates opening into a walled compound. Through them he caught a glimpse of flowerpots laid out in rows under the shade of some ancient olive trees and he ran towards them.

Mr Hasbini, ignoring the familiar rumble and stutter of fighting two miles away in the town, had been squatting on the hot hard ground in the middle of his nursery garden slicing geranium stems and sticking them into pots full of freshly watered soil. He stood up, grumbling as his knees creaked, then pushed back his broken straw hat and scratched his bald head as he surveyed his long rows of pots.

'I'm a silly old fool,' he remarked to his pigeons, who were dozing through the midday heat in their cages under the shade of an old fig tree. 'Why do I bother? Who wants pot plants when there's a war on?'

He raised his head as he heard a distant rumble and frowned. 'Still miles away,' he said, 'but coming this way. I'd better close up in case.'

He was about to go and shut the gates when the boy ran through them into the compound. Mr Hasbini picked up a spade and shook it at him.

'Get out of here!' he shouted.

'It's all right,' panted the boy. 'It's me, Sami. You know me, Mr Hasbini. I used to come here with my dad to buy plants . . .'

'Sami? Mr Faris's son?' Mr Hasbini looked at the boy in astonishment.

'We've got to get out of here,' the boy said, dancing with impatience. 'There are tanks coming up the road. We'll be trapped!'

71

'And where do you suggest we go?' Mr Hasbini had rested his spade on the ground and was leaning on it. 'Up the road, into the battle in the middle of town? Or down the road towards the tanks?'

'Across the fields, through the orchards . . .'

'Don't be daft, boy. They're mined. No, we're going to stay here. Safest place to be. The tanks won't bother us. They're making for those hotheads up in town. Stop jumping up and down. You're giving me a headache. Tell me what on earth you're doing here on your own. Where are your parents?'

The boy shook back his tousled black hair and hitched up his trousers, which had grown too loose on his scrawny waist and fell in folds over his torn trainers.

'They went to my grandma's village, but I ran away. I've been on my own for weeks. I can't go till I've found Ramzi.'

'Your older brother? How did you come to lose him?'

'We were at school when it was bombed. The whole building collapsed. I got out all right, but Ramzi . . . He *must* have escaped! I *know* he did! But no one will believe me. Everyone just says . . .'

'Checked the hospitals, did you?' said Mr Hasbini.

'Yes. He's not in any of them.'

'In that case . . .' Mr Hasbini began.

'I know what you're thinking,' interrupted Sami, his newly broken voice suddenly high-pitched with anger, 'but it's not true! Plenty of boys got out. I saw them.

72

There was shooting everywhere just after the bomb, and I ran away. I hid for hours till the fighting stopped, and when I went back I couldn't find Ramzi. I went home, and Dad said we had to go to the village, but I wouldn't go. Not without Ramzi. Dad shouted at me, but I wouldn't go. I've been hunting and hunting . . .'

His voice shook and he wiped his forearm across his dirt-smeared face. Mr Hasbini stopped looking at him and squatted down among his flowerpots.

'What are you doing?' said Sami after a while.

Mr Hasbini dusted earth off his hands and sliced through another geranium stem.

'Taking geranium cuttings, of course. Didn't they teach you anything at that school? These bits of stalk will grow into new plants. They'll be a picture next year.'

'Huh! Next year!' the boy squatted down beside him. 'We'll all be bombed to bits next year.'

'You probably will be if you keep on running round town in the middle of a civil war,' remarked Mr Hasbini. 'But these cuttings will still grow. It won't make any difference if we're dead or not. They'll just put out roots and leaves and turn into brand new plants.'

'So what?' Sami picked up a geranium leaf and crushed it between his fingers.

'Stop that! Where's your respect for nature?'

'I don't care about nature. Nature's a waste of time.'

'A waste of time?' Mr Hasbini cast his eyes up to heaven. 'Do you know which side's going to win this war?'

'Our side is. My dad says . . .'

'Rubbish. Nobody's going to win. Have you seen that supermarket that was bombed last year? There are trees growing right through the tarmac in the car park, and grass and flowers sprouting all over the ruins. Nature's going to win this war, that's what. Nature always wins.'

'Listen. The tanks are coming,' said Sami, lifting his head.

'Never mind the tanks. They don't mind about us,' said Mr Hasbini. Carefully, he pushed another geranium stem into the waiting earth.

Sami picked up the knife.

'Can I do one?' he asked.

'Yes, but take care. Don't bruise it. Look, I'll show you . . .'

They both jumped suddenly as a burst of automatic rifle fire came from the direction of the town but quite close by. It ripped through the air. Mr Hasbini struggled quickly to his feet.

'That was close! Quick, help me shut the gates!'

Sami was at the gates in an instant, clanging the first one shut. Mr Hasbini ran after him, his stiff legs working as fast as they could. The tanks had nearly arrived outside the nursery garden. Their huge caterpillar wheels clanked over the tarmac. They had stopped at the sound of gunfire, and their still deafening engines were idling.

'Would you believe it! Those madmen are attacking the tanks!' panted Mr Hasbini as he shut the second gate and plunged the bolts home.

For a moment, they both relaxed. The nursery garden looked peaceful, enclosed in its high wall. Except for the pigeons, who were fluttering with fright in their cages, it was almost impossible to believe that a battle was about to break out just outside.

But the ambush was only a few hundred metres away. Sami could even hear the men's voices as they broke cover, frantic questions and hoarse shouts of command.

'Can't stay here,' said Mr Hasbini. 'Gate's too flimsy. Bullets'll rip right through it,' and he began to run again, gasping for breath, towards the small concrete shed in the middle of the garden.

Automatically, Sami followed him. Then he saw where Mr Hasbini was going.

Not inside, he thought. Not trapped inside!

He looked round desperately. His instinct was to run, but there was nowhere safe to go. The pigeons were flapping their wings and pecking violently at the wire of their cages. Sami ran to them.

'Sami! Come here! What are you doing?' Mr Hasbini shouted, but Sami did not listen. He was fumbling with the latches of the cages.

'Get out! Fly away!' he shouted as he wrenched the doors open. 'You'll be trapped, you stupid birds! Get out!'

The pigeons, more terrified than ever, fluttered away from him into the backs of their cages.

'Sami! Over here!' called Mr Hasbini. Sami looked round. Mr Hasbini was not inside the shed but behind it, crouching against its concrete wall.

The noise of the battle was deafening now. Sami could not see the men running down the road directly outside the compound, but he could hear the clatter of their feet and the sharp cracks of their rifles as they let off rounds of automatic fire. He felt the dreadful trembling weakness of terror engulf him as he dropped down beside the old man.

'I'd rather be outside at a time like this,' said Mr Hasbini. 'If I'm going to die, I'd rather do it with the sky above me, looking at my garden.'

Sami nodded. In spite of the heat, he was shivering.

'I was in the science lab when the roof fell in,' he said. 'I was near the window. I only just got out. I couldn't find Ramzi. He was in the library. It was . . .' He stopped, his lips trembling, then went on again. 'I've been hunting for three weeks, going round the hospitals, going to his friends' places, looking everywhere he might have run to if he was really scared.'

Mr Hasbini grunted.

'Why are you so sure he's still alive?'

'He's got to be! How can I be alive, and not Ramzi?'

With a deafening bang, a mortar hit the ground on the far side of the shed and exploded, splintering flowerpots and throwing earth and cuttings in all directions. Sami flinched, and covered his head with his arms.

There was a moment of eerie silence, as if the whole world was waiting. And then the tank opened fire. The six-inch shell flew over the compound wall with a deafening roar, screamed across the garden and ploughed through the wall on the far side with a bang that seemed to make the very air shake. It set the echoes flying.

Sami and Mr Hasbini had shrunk into themselves. They were squatting against the concrete wall of the shed with their arms tightly wrapped round their knees, making themselves as small as possible. Sami was rocking backwards and forwards, and in the silence that followed the explosion, Mr Hasbini heard him whimpering. Not knowing what to say or how to comfort him, he began awkwardly to pat his shoulder, tears running down his own weather-beaten cheeks.

'Ramzi's dead, isn't he?' Sami said at last. 'You think he's dead.'

'Yes,' said Mr Hasbini.

Sami looked at him as if he was seeing him for the first time.

'We'll all be dead soon. What does it matter?' he cried suddenly, jumping to his feet. 'Why bother to take cover? What's the point? Kill me too, go on, get me too!' and before Mr Hasbini could stop him, he had run out from the shelter of the concrete wall and was standing unprotected in the open garden.

'Go on! Shoot me!' he shrieked at the sky, and he flung out his arms, put his head back and shut his eyes.

Nothing happened. Quietness had suddenly fallen. The battle outside was over. The only sound was the rumbling of the tanks' great caterpillar wheels as they started rolling on again up the road towards the town.

Sami opened his eyes.

'I'm alive!' he said aloud. 'Ramzi's dead, and I'm alive.'

He felt very tired and a little dizzy. He sat down on the ground.

'You certainly won't be alive much longer if you go on doing that kind of thing,' said Mr Hasbini disapprovingly as he came out from behind the shed. 'Scared me more than the tanks.'

He looked round his garden. The shell had blown a big hole in one wall and torn a branch off a tree, but most of the flowerpots still stood in their neat rows. The pigeons, who had taken off and flown around in a high circle while the battle raged, had come back to peck and strut round the grain bowls in their cages.

'See what I mean?' said Mr Hasbini with a rare smile. 'Nature always wins.'

'I want to go home, to Mum and Dad,' said Sami suddenly, rising shakily to his feet.

'That's not a bad idea. As a matter of fact, I think I'll come with you. I could do with a few days of peace and quiet. We'll wait till it's dark. It'll be safer then. In the meantime, let's eat. I've got some food in my shed. I expect you're hungry. Boys usually are.'

Sami nodded. Suddenly he was ravenous.

'I'll only stay away for a day or two, mind,' went on Mr Hasbini. 'I'll have to get back to mend that hole in the wall and do my watering, if the water's still turned on, and feed the birds.'

'I'll come with you,' said Sami. 'I'll help you.'

'Maybe,' said Mr Hasbini. He turned towards his shed. 'Come back in the spring, anyway. You won't believe your eyes. Those little bits of stalk will be great big geranium plants, all scarlet and orange and pink, and the cuts that made them will be quite forgotten. The world will be like a new place then. You'll see.'

The Crocodile and the Cassowary Bird

A story from Papua New Guinea

In the jungles of New Guinea, there was once a cassowary bird who lived near a river. He had planted a sago tree, and he was waiting for the trunk to fill with sago, so that he could cut it down and eat it.

It's nearly ready, he told himself one day. Tomorrow I'll cut the leaves off the top, and the trunk will grow even fatter as the sago swells inside.

But that evening, a crocodile floated down the river. He saw the sago tree, and smiled to himself.

That is a very fine tree, he thought, and it doesn't seem to belong to anyone. The leaves should be cut off the top, and the trunk will fill up with even more sago. I'd like a good meal of sago. I'll climb up there and do it myself.

So the crocodile scrambled out of the river and up the bank to the tree. He found a post nearby, leaned it against the trunk and crawled up it till he reached the top. Then he began cutting off the leaves.

Just then, the cassowary bird came by.

'You wicked crocodile!' he shouted. 'What are you doing in my sago tree? I'll punish you for this!'

And he pulled away the post.

The crocodile was trapped now. He was stranded up the tree, a prisoner of the cassowary bird. All he could do was begin to eat away at the sago inside the trunk of the tree.

He began to munch at it, and he munched and munched, a bit at a time, day after day, week after week, right down the inside of the tree, until at last, three whole months after he had climbed the tree, he ate a mouthful of mud, and realised he had reached the earth at the bottom. Then he chewed a hole in the side of the tree and came out on to the river bank at last.

He dived into the river at once, longing for a swim and a long, cool drink, but because he had eaten nothing but sago for such a long time, he was light and thin and could only float on the surface of the water.

Just then, the crocodile saw the cassowary bird strutting by. I'll have my revenge on him, he thought, and he swam quietly to the river bank and snatched the cassowary bird up in his mouth. The cassowary had only time for one loud squawk before he was dragged out into the middle of the river.

'Don't kill me, please!' panted the cassowary bird.

'I won't,' said the crocodile, 'but I'm going to keep you prisoner for as long as you kept me.'

For three months the crocodile kept the cassowary bird prisoner in his dark damp den in the river bank, until the cassowary was thin and hungry and longing to be free. Then the crocodile let him go.

'One creature should not catch another and imprison him,' the crocodile said sternly to the cassowary bird.

'Oh yes, yes, I agree,' the cassowary said nervously, and he scurried off into the jungle, before the crocodile could catch him again.

Skippy

I always play the same game when I'm walking home from school. You might say I was a bit old for this kind of thing, but I've done it since I was a little kid, and I sort of like it.

What I do is touch the fence on the right of the pavement, then zigzag across to touch one of the parked cars, then back to the fence, then across to another car, or skip, or van, or whatever, then the fence and so on, all the way down the street. I make sure no one's looking, though.

Anyway, I was doing this one day, as usual, when I heard this funny noise. It was a scrabbling, scratching sort of noise.

I looked up and down and all around but there was

nothing above me (except the sky, of course), or on the pavement (except for some blobs of ancient flattened-out chewing gum). And the houses all looked the same as usual (except for number forty-nine, which was covered with scaffolding).

Then I heard it again, a sort of sk-rr-schtt-skr-tch noise. I realised that it was coming from the skip I'd just passed. It had to be. So I went up to the skip and looked inside.

It was empty, except for one thing. A crocodile.

OK, I know it's hard to believe, but you've just got to try. I'm telling you, right there, in that skip, large as life, there was a crocodile.

It was quite a small one, as crocodiles go – only about a metre long – and it had knobbly skin and short, bulgy legs and its eyes were all green and glittery.

The crocodile was trying to scramble up the sloping end of the skip, but every time it got halfway up, it slid down to the bottom again.

Well, as you can imagine, I thought I'd entered another world, or slipped into the fourth dimension or something. So I looked all around again in case there were aliens or wizards or time machines hanging around. There weren't of course. But when I looked back down into the skip, the crocodile was still there. It was trying to heave itself up the side again, slowly and painfully. It only got a little way up before it slid helplessly back down to the bottom.

It seemed to give up then. It lay, looking up at me, all sort of pathetic.

I know what you're thinking. You're thinking that crocodiles are fierce and scary and dangerous and couldn't possibly look pathetic. But this one did.

'You'll tire yourself out,' I said to it. 'How long have you been in there, anyway? Hey, you haven't passed out or anything, have you? Wave a claw, or blink or something. Hm. You don't look very well to me.'

Good thing no one was passing at that precise moment. They'd have thought I was a total nutter, leaning into a skip and chatting away to a crocodile.

Then I heard a clatter and a shout from the house with all the scaffolding. A builder had stuck his head out of one of the windows.

'Excuse me,' I called out, running back towards him. 'Did you know that there's a crocodile in that skip over there?'

The builder just looked at me the way they do when they think you're messing them about.

'You what?' he said nastily.

'There's a crocodile. A live one. In the skip. Honestly,' I said.

He just scowled at me.

'Get out of here, you little devil,' he growled, 'before I come down and give you a clip round the ear-hole.'

And he pulled his head inside the window again.

So I went back to the skip, hoping but not hoping that I'd imagined it all, if you know what I mean. The crocodile was still there. It looked sicker than ever, its head drooping down on to the hot metal of the skip floor, all parched and exhausted and miserable.

You know what my problem is? Act first, think afterwards. I've been like that all my life, ever since I was a toddler in my pushchair and I offered my first ice cream to a dog to let it have a lick. So now, instead of doing something sensible, like walking away, or fetching someone, I dropped my bag on the pavement, hoisted one leg over the side of the skip, then the other, and a second later, I was standing there right beside the crocodile.

Only then did I remember all the things you see on telly programmes – crocodiles looking dead and boring, pretending to be logs, then suddenly coming to life and going for their prey with the speed of light. What do they do next? Rip off your arm or leg before you can say 'gotcha'.

This crocodile's teeth, the ones sticking up out of his lower jaw, they looked – well, put it this way, the thought of them sinking into any bit of me made me suddenly go all cold and sweaty.

It's amazing, isn't it, what your mind will do in a crisis? Mine whizzed round so fast that it brought out a fact I never knew I knew. Here it is. Crocodiles have super powerful jaws when it comes to biting down on things, but really weedy muscles when it comes to opening their mouths again. So it's quite easy to hold a crocodile's mouth shut. People even do it with their bare hands.

Moving really slowly, I worked off my school tie and

made a sort of noose out of it. Then I shut my eyes for a second, wished myself tons and tons of luck, and sprang.

Well, there was no way that poor little crocodile was going to try and bite me. He looked half dead, to be honest. It was really easy, slipping the loop of my tie over his long snout, and easing it gently into place so it fitted snugly.

Now that his jaws were safely locked together, I started to feel a whole lot safer. The croc looked awful though, all limp and hopeless.

'Don't worry, Skippy,' I told him. (The right name for him had come to me, just like that.) 'I'm going to get you out of here. You'll be all right. Trust me. Just don't go and die first, OK?'

It's not the easiest thing in the world, heaving a metre-long crocodile out of a skip, when you're not all that tall yourself. How I managed it, I'll never know. There was a nasty moment when I was balancing on the edge and the croc came to life and lashed his tail and nearly knocked me flying, but I just said, 'Come on, you idiot, whose side do you think I'm on?' and he sort of lost heart again.

A minute later, there I was, standing on the pavement, with my schoolbag over my shoulder and a large reptile in my arms, not having a clue what to do next.

Then I saw, stumping along the road, old Mrs Fitcham, the street busybody, and I thought, Do I want Mrs Fitcham asking me a million questions about why

I'm standing here holding a crocodile? I do not.

So I legged it home.

I'll have to go back a bit at this point and explain that it was a Thursday. My mum works late on a Thursday and I have to let myself into the house. Granddad comes round later on to do my tea and keep me company. That's the official story, anyway. Usually, I do most of the tea, and it's me keeping Granddad company. He's lived alone since Grandma died, and he's got a bad heart, and Mum worries about him a lot.

'Don't get up to anything tonight,' she says every Thursday morning. 'Shocks aren't good for him. He mightn't pull through the next heart attack, you know.'

It wasn't until I'd got home and rung the doorbell, and no one had answered, and I'd fished out my key, and opened the door, and gone inside, and called out for Mum, and she hadn't answered, that I remembered it was Thursday.

It was a bit of a blow, quite frankly. It's not that I don't like Granddad. I do. He's brilliant. But the thought of him coming face to face with Skippy, and clutching his chest, and going blue, and falling down dead and it being all my fault made my hair stand on end.

It was still only four o'clock though. Granddad wasn't due till 5.30. I had a whole hour and a half to sort things out. And the first thing that needed sorting out was saving poor old Skippy's life.

You don't need to be a world-class genius to know that

crocodiles like water. And it was only one small step from there to imagining him paddling happily round in the bath. So I carted him upstairs, lowered him gently in, put in the plug and turned on the cold tap. Then I pulled my tie off his snout.

You could practically see the little guy sigh with relief and pleasure. He eased himself slowly along the sides of the bath, sort of exploring it. As the water crept up his sides, he lifted his chin (if you can call it that) and lowered it again, opening his mouth to let the water trickle in.

'Supper next, Skip,' I said. 'I bet you're starving.'

The only thing was, I didn't know exactly the sorts of things that crocodiles like to eat. Except for raw zebra and antelope and human being, of course, but there weren't any of those in the fridge, as I knew to my certain knowledge.

There was only a packet of fish fingers. They were meant for Granddad's and my supper. I'd seen them when I'd got out the milk for breakfast.

Fish, I thought, looking down at Skippy. I bet you like fish. It's worth a try, anyway.

I was down the stairs and up again in a flash, and a minute later I was dangling the first fish finger in front of the crocodile's nose.

Big mistake. With a lunge so fast you couldn't see him move, he'd snatched the fish finger and practically taken my fingers off with it.

'Right,' I said. 'I get the message. You like fish.'

I dropped the next fish finger into the bath. He snapped it up at once. And the next. And the next. A couple of moments later, the whole packet had gone.

I looked at my watch. I still had time to run down to the parade and buy more fish fingers, but first I had some calls to make.

I just stood there looking at the phone for about a million years, not knowing who to call. Then I remembered what Grandma always used to say.

'When in doubt, call a policeman.'

So I dialled 999. The woman answered so quickly that I wasn't ready.

'Fire, police or ambulance?' she rapped out.

'Er, I don't know,' I said.

'Well? What's the problem?

'There's a crocodile in my bath.'

'A what?'

'A crocodile, and I'm scared my granddad's going to come and find it and have a heart attack.'

'Now look here, sonny,' she went, going all frosty on me. 'Making hoax calls to the emergency services is an offence. Get off the line.'

And she put the phone down on me.

I was disappointed. I suppose I thought they'd have sent a fire engine round, or a police car, at least. That would have been great, that would.

And then light dawned. Of course! The zoo! They'd know what to do.

I got out the phone book and dialled the number.

'For the latest information on opening times,' the voice said, 'visit our website. If you have a touchtone telephone . . .'

I was about to give up, when a real voice broke in.

'Hello,' a man said. 'Can I help you?'

'Yes please,' I said. 'I've found a crocodile. In a skip. It wasn't very well. I've brought it home and now it's in my bath. Can you come and take it away quick before my Granddad gets here? He's got a bad heart and the shock might kill him.'

The man didn't seem interested in my granddad.

'Reptile rescue, that's what you need,' he said, sounding bored. 'Can't put you through just now. They feed the snakes on Thursdays. Call back tomorrow.'

And then the line went dead.

For a moment I nearly panicked. I nearly ran outside into the street shouting 'Help! Crocodile alert! Emergency! Fire! Reptiles!' But I didn't. I just stayed brilliantly calm.

RSPCA, I thought. They rescue dogs and badgers and stuff. I've seen them on the telly.

I was thumbing through the phone book, looking for their number, when I heard someone whistling. It was Granddad! Nearly an hour early! Coming to the front door!

I could feel my hair standing on end. What should I do? Haul Skippy out of the bath and hide him under my bed?

Useless. He'd crawl out. Tell Granddad he didn't need to stay because I was going round to my friend Luke's? Hopeless. He'd come in anyway and wait for me to get back home.

He was practically at the door by now. I could hear the change jingling in his pocket as he fished around for his key. All I had time to do was bolt upstairs and shut the bathroom door.

I whizzed up the stairs, slammed the door shut and raced down again at approx. the speed of light, and was back in the hall by the time he'd got himself inside.

'Hello there, Jack,' he said. 'Climbed any beanstalks recently?'

He always says stuff like that.

I took his coat off him and hung it up and tried to lure him into the sitting room.

'Come and put your feet up,' I said, all concerned. 'You look tired out.'

'In a minute, Jack, in a minute,' he said. 'Got to go to the toilet first,' and he started up the stairs.

My heart actually stopped beating. That's what it felt like, anyway.

What would Granddad do when he'd been to the toilet? He'd wash his hands. Where would he wash his hands? In the bathroom. What would he see when he opened the bathroom door? A crocodile. Would he or would he not have a heart attack? He would.

And I hadn't a clue what to do about it.

I followed him up the stairs and waited. Then I heard the toilet flush. I stood outside the bathroom door, trying to look desperately keen and eager.

'Come on downstairs, Granddad,' I said. 'I want to show you something. It's – it's my school project. On the Tudors. It's brilliant.'

'All in good time,' he wheezed. 'Got to wash my hands first,' and he tried to move past me to the bathroom door.

I nipped in front of him and took hold of his arm.

'You don't want to go in there, Granddad,' I said. 'The basin's all bunged up. It's full of dirty water that won't go down the plughole. Drain's blocked or something.'

'Really?' He was looking keen. 'Has your mum got a plunger, by any chance? I'll have a go at it for you.'

That's the trouble with my granddad. He loves it when stuff like that happens. If my bike gets a puncture, or a leg falls off the table, or someone busts a window, he's in there right away doing his DIY. He only ever makes things worse though.

I realised too late that I'd made a horrible mistake.

'It's OK, Granddad.' I was thinking furiously. 'The plumber's coming in the morning. Mum said, if you want to get stuck in, the back door needs mending. It's sticking and the handle keeps coming off.'

What she'd actually said was, 'Do me a favour, love. Don't let him get started on the house. Specially not the back door. It's bad enough as it is.'

'Anyway,' I said, biting my lips, '*Battleaxe* has just

started on the telly. You could settle in. I'll get you a cup of tea if you like.'

He was tempted, I could tell, but the thought of the door was too much for him. He set off down the stairs.

'Nah. I like to make myself useful.' He'd already opened the cupboard under the stairs and was rooting around behind the old curtains and pots of paint Mum keeps in there. 'Yes, I thought as much. The toolkit's still here where I left it last time after I had a go at that duff window. Now then. Let me see. What do I need . . .'

He was muttering away happily to himself. I wiped the sweat off my forehead. He'd be busy for ages now. With a bit of luck, I'd be able to keep him going till Mum came home. I'd hand the whole problem over to her.

And then I heard that sound again, coming from upstairs.

Sk-rr-schtt-skr-tch.

My blood practically froze. I knew at once what it meant. Skippy was trying to climb out of the bath. All those fish fingers and the nice drink of water had revved him up again. He was making a break for freedom.

There's only one thing for it, I said to myself. I've got to get him out of here.

I don't know if you've ever tried to smuggle a metre-long crocodile, who's gone hyper on fish fingers, out of the house under the nose of your old granddad? Believe me. It's a nightmare.

Now just keep calm, I told myself. And think. Calm. That's right. Cool. Think.

So I thought. And then I remembered my old sports bag. It was one of those long narrow ones that you can put cricket bats and stuff into. It was the perfect shape for a crocodile.

Quick as quick, I raced upstairs, fished the bag out from the back of my cupboard, made a noose again with my tie, crept into the bathroom, lassoed Skippy round the snout, lifted him out of the bath (he kept thrashing his tail around and I got totally soaked), stuck him in the bag, did up the zip, changed into a dry sweatshirt, thought up a story for Granddad, and went back downstairs again, carrying Skippy in the bag.

'Er, Granddad,' I said, sticking my head into the kitchen. 'I've just remembered. Mum said she'd forgotten to get us any supper. She told me to go up the shops and buy us some fish fingers.'

He hardly bothered to look up. He'd unscrewed the lock from the back door and taken it to bits. Screws and things were lying all over the step, and he was looking down at them, scratching his head.

'Yes, OK, see you in a minute,' he said. 'Now then. This clips onto here, and that screw ought to . . . No. this washer goes . . .'

I left him to it.

I was out of the house and halfway down the street, still sweating with relief, when I realised that I didn't know what I was going to do. I didn't want to put poor old Skippy back into his skip. Those horrible builders would be bound to chuck half a ton of rubbish all over him without even knowing he was there.

'When in doubt,' I heard Grandma's voice again, 'ask a . . .'

Yes, but the police didn't help much when I tried them last time, I told her in my head.

Still, it was an idea. The only one on offer, anyway. So I started walking a bit quicker, and then broke into a trot. The police station was a good ten minutes away. I'd have to whizz if I didn't want Granddad to start getting worried.

Skippy was as good as gold. You'd have thought he wouldn't have liked being bounced around in a smelly old sports bag, but he just lay there, all quiet and still, while I zoomed along the pavement towards the police station.

I'd never been in there before. It wasn't the way I'd expected at all. There was just this counter, and a bored looking copper leaning on it, without a cap on or anything, drinking a mug of tea.

'What's up with you then?' he said. 'Someone nicked your skateboard?'

'No,' I panted. 'I've got something for you,' and I opened the bag, lifted out Skippy, and put him down on the counter.

The policeman went, 'Oi, what on earth . . .?' and jumped backwards. Maybe that was what upset

Skippy. He started lashing out with his tail. With the first swish, the copper's mug of tea went flying. The second swish knocked a pile of notices off the counter. The third swish –

But I didn't wait to see what the third swish would do. I reckoned I was in enough trouble already. I leaned forward and gave Skippy one last pat on his leathery, knobbly back.

'Good luck,' I said, then I turned and bolted, out through the doors, down the steps, and away along the street.

It wasn't until I'd belted round the corner into our own street, and was almost at our house, that I remembered I hadn't stopped to get the fish fingers.

I nearly turned to dash back to the shops, when Granddad opened the front door. He was looking worried.

'There you are, Jack,' he said. 'I was just beginning to wonder where you'd got to.'

'Sorry,' I said. 'They were out of fish fingers at the corner shop. I had to run up to the high street. They hadn't got any there, either. We'll have to have beans on toast.'

'Oh, that's all right.' He turned back into the house. 'I'm always up for beans on toast. And I've got the back door to shut. Only problem is, it won't open now. You'll have to get someone in to see to it. And I've had a look at the basin in the bathroom. Seems fine to me. There's a terrible mess up there, though. Water and towels everywhere. It looks like a wild animal's been wrecking the place.'

'Don't worry, Granddad,' I said. 'I'll clear it up. Now how about that cup of tea?'

You'd have thought, wouldn't you, that I'd have slept like a log that night, all relieved and exhausted, but I didn't get a wink. I'd remembered, you see, that I'd left my tie wrapped round Skippy's nose. My school tie. With the school badge on it. All the police would need to do, if they wanted to find out who'd planted a dangerous wild animal in their police station, would be to come round to the school and check if anyone had lost a tie.

It wasn't until it was getting light that I remembered my old tie, the one spattered with paint stains, that was stuffed in the back of a drawer.

It wasn't just me I was worried about though. It was Skippy, too. I mean, would the police be nice to him? Would they understand about giving him water and fish fingers? Or would they sort of arrest him, and lock him up in a cell and leave him there?

It was a relief, I can tell you, when I came home from school a couple of days later, and saw the local freebie newspaper lying on the mat.

'Wildlife smuggler arrested,' it said, in banner headlines. 'Mr Jolyon Plummer, 42, has been arrested in a bizarre case involving exotic animals. Unknown to his neighbours, Mr Plummer, an alleged wildlife smuggler and unemployed dog beautician, has been keeping large numbers of dangerous rare animals at his home at 16 Sycamore Gardens. Learning that the police had been tipped off and were about to raid his premises, Mr Plummer allegedly panicked and tried to dump the animals. A parrot has been rescued from a telephone box, a pair of tarantulas were found in a public toilet, and two boa constrictors were discovered in a bus shelter by local resident Mrs Fitcham, 74. They reportedly gave her a nasty turn but no lasting damage was done. Finally, a crocodile was delivered safe and well by a public-spirited schoolboy, whose name has not been released by the police. The crocodile has found a new home at the zoo, and is said to be settling in well.

'The deplorable trade in smuggled exotic pets, which causes great suffering to animals and adversely affects the populations in the wild, is the subject of our leader on page . . .'

I didn't bother to read any more. A weight had dropped off my shoulders.

'Yesss!' I shouted, punching the air. 'Good old Skippy! Good old me, too!'

I'd thought no one was in the house, but Mum came out of the kitchen.

'What's up with you?' she said.

I nearly told her. I wanted to, but I didn't think she'd believe me. I hardly believed it myself.

'Nothing,' I said. 'What's for supper?'

'Fish fingers,' she said. 'OK?'

The Bear and the Woman

A story from Ethiopia

Once upon a time, the bear and the woman were friends. They were good neighbours. They shared things, and knew each other's ways.

One day, when the woman was cooking porridge, she saw that her water pot was empty.

I'll run to the river, she thought, and fill my pot. If I'm quick, my porridge won't have time to burn.

The bear was standing outside her hut.

'Are you cooking porridge?' he asked. 'It smells very good.'

The woman didn't look at him.

If I tell him about my porridge, he'll want to share it with me but I want to eat it all myself, she thought.

'Porridge?' she replied. 'What porridge?' and she pushed past the bear and ran down to the river.

The bear sniffed the air again. The porridge smelled wonderful and he was hungry. He looked into the woman's hut and saw the porridge bubbling away in its pot on the fire.

I'll just taste a little bit, he thought, and he pulled the spoon out of the porridge pot and licked it.

'Mm,' he said to himself. 'I'll try a little more.'

So he ate some more, and then some more, and some after that . . .

The woman came home and found the bear scraping the last spoonful of porridge out of her pot.

'You wicked bear! You've eaten all my porridge!' she shouted furiously. She picked up a big stick and hit him on the head.

The bear roared with pain and fear. He ran out of the woman's hut towards her donkey. It was tethered with a rope to a tree.

The donkey brayed in terror when he saw the bear.

The bear wants to eat me! he thought. He pulled at his rope until it broke, and then he ran away.

The rope shook the tree and dislodged a nest of bees, which smashed down on to the ground. The maddened bees swarmed out of it.

'Someone's attacking us!' they buzzed.

Looking round, they saw a chicken, which belonged to the chief, who lived nearby. They flew up to the chicken and began to sting her.

'Stop! Stop!' squawked the chicken. 'You're hurting me!'

And she lifted her head and flapped her wings.

The wind from her wings caught the grains of wheat, which the chief's wife was drying on a mat near her door, and blew them all away.

The chief's wife ran out of her hut.

'You stupid chicken!' she cried. 'Why are you flapping your wings?'

'The bees were stinging me,' said the chicken, 'and it hurt.'

'Why did you sting my chicken?' the chief's wife asked the bees.

'Our nest fell out of the tree when the donkey pulled his rope,' explained the bees. 'We thought we were being attacked.'

'Why did you pull your rope?' the chief's wife asked the donkey.

'The bear ran at me, roaring,' said the donkey, 'and I was afraid.'

'Why did you roar and run at the donkey?' the chief's wife asked the bear.

'The woman hit me with her stick,' said the bear. 'I was running away from her.'

'Why did you hit the bear with your stick?' the chief's wife asked the woman.

'The bear came into my house and ate all my porridge,' said the woman, 'and I was very hungry.'

'Ah,' said the chief's wife. 'I see. Let's take this problem to the chief.'

So everyone went to see the chief. He listened to them carefully.

'The bear is greedy,' he said. 'He likes to eat other people's food. But the woman is selfish. She doesn't like to share. They can no longer live together. One of them must go away.'

So the bear went to live in the forest. He didn't want to go. He was angry with the woman. He lives there still, and his anger has never died. The woman knows this, and she

105

is frightened of the bear, and of all wild creatures. Whenever she finds them in her house, she drives them out with blows of her stick.

Lord of the Garden

The afternoon heat had been stifling. The sun was still beating down relentlessly on the French countryside, baking the yellow stones of the old church, and making the cluster of houses on the hill shimmer in its brilliant light.

It had been too hot for people and animals alike. No one had crossed the dusty square to the empty café. No one had driven down the winding lane between the fields of yellow stubble and ripe sunflowers. The one-eyed cat in the overgrown garden below the old church tower lay asleep in the shade of the apple tree. Even the mice, who had taken over the derelict house to which the garden belonged, stayed quietly in the cool of the stone-floored kitchen.

And then, as the afternoon moved into evening, a breeze fluttered across the woods and the stream. It wafted through the stone mullions of the church tower and ruffled the feathers of the owl, whose head had been buried in sleep under its wing.

The owl looked up. He was alone up here. He had dozed all day through the heat, and the breeze came as a relief. He spread his wings and made a flying hop to land on the ancient oak beam, as thick as a man's waist, which ran from one side of the tower to the other. One of his talons flicked against the bell which hung from the beam. It gave out a faint, musical clang, which vibrated for a moment in the air.

From the far side of the valley, came the sound of a car engine. The owl blinked and turned his wide face. He saw the flash of glass and metal as a car sped down to the bridge. He watched it climb the hill towards the village. A moment later it turned into the empty square and rolled to a stop at the gate of the deserted garden.

Voices broke into the silence as the car doors burst open and two children and their parents jumped out.

'Hey, Didi, look, there's an apple tree in the garden,' the boy said. 'Bet you can't climb it.'

'Bet I can.'

The little girl had already opened the gate. Its rusty hinge squeaked. The cat, roused from sleep, pattered confidently towards her. It writhed around her feet, mewing loudly.

The owl had ignored the human voices but at the sound of his old enemy, the cat, he hopped to a rafter in the roof of the tower. From here he had a perfect view of the garden through one of the mullions.

'Oh, what a dear little cat!' Didi said. 'What's wrong with its eye?'

'Don't touch it!' her mother said sharply. 'It looks diseased. It'll have fleas, anyway.'

The father had been feeling about under the red tiled eaves of the cottage which hung down low over the door. With a grunt of triumph, he pulled out a key.

'I told you! I said it would still be here.'

He tried to fit it into the rusty lock.

'The whole place has gone to rack and ruin,' his wife said, standing back and frowning at the house. 'What on earth gave you the idea that we could actually sleep here?'

The key grated noisily as it turned in the lock. The man looked back at her defensively.

'Poor Maman,' he said. 'She struggled on here long after she could really manage. We ought to have come more often. Anyway, now that the place is ours, we can . . .'

Their voices faded as they disappeared into the house.

The cat stretched out its front legs, scarred with old battle wounds. Then it trotted to the doorstep of the cottage and sat on it, wrapping its tail proudly around its paws. Already it looked bolder, pleased with itself, pleased to be with humans again.

The watching owl felt the feathers that edged his round face stand out in a bristle of hostility. The deserted garden, with its overgrown currant bushes, its dahlias lost in a sea of thistles, and its lettuces, long since gone to seed, had been *his* hunting ground. Its bounty had kept him and his mate supplied all through the last two summers. Together they had reared two broods of owlets. Together, they had been a match for the cat.

But since his mate had gone to her death, three months ago, under the wheels of a speeding van, the owl had lost the will to fight. He had been driven further afield, forced to fly out to the hedgerows and fields across the valley for the more meagre pickings of the open country.

The door of the cottage below was suddenly flung open and the woman ran out.

'Mice everywhere! This is the last straw! Dust all over everything, plaster falling off the walls! Why can't we get a holiday place near the sea like everyone else?'

The man appeared in the doorway.

'It'll be all right when we've cleaned it up. The children love it already. Anyway, stop fussing about the mice. They're easy enough to deal with. I'll put poison down for them tomorrow.'

Evening was falling now. The light had already faded from the valley and shadows were creeping steadily up the hillsides. Only the church tower was now fully lit by the setting sun.

The owl preened his feathers. There was a good hour to wait before it would be dark enough to hunt.

The sounds of evening came clearly through the mullions to strike his sensitive ears. A dog was barking down by the pond at the splash of a jumping trout. Cows, heavy with milk, were mooing impatiently at the farm gate. A cawing of crows and thrumming of wood pigeons rose from the woods beyond the village. The air below the tower was filled with the beat of swallows' wings as they soared and dived after their insect prey. Somewhere, a mile away, a car changed gear as it climbed a hill. Down below, in the cottage, doors creaked open and shut, furniture was being pulled about and the children's voices were raised in excited quarrels.

The lights in the village flickered on one by one. The air was cooler now. The breeze had stiffened and wisps of high cloud were veiling the rising moon.

The owl perched on the stone embrasure and cocked his head. He had picked up a rustle in the garden below. He could hear some small creature moving through the brittle old leaves under the apple tree. The owl shifted from one foot to the other, ready to swoop down, but even in the darkness his penetrating eyes could see the long black shape of the cat, lurking under the broken seat where once the old lady had sat. It was waiting for him, as it always did. He would have to hunt in the fields again tonight.

He took off, gliding over the cottage, his pale wings a blur of white against the dark sky. Then he screeched out his harsh hunting cry. The sound made the mice scamper in fear and the one-eyed cat lifted its head to watch its enemy. The family in the house, eating their first meal in the dusty kitchen, held their forks still in their hands and stared at each other.

'It's a ghost!' said Didi, shivering. 'Something from the cemetery, out of one of the graves. It's coming . . .'

'Shut up!' her brother said savagely.

The owl had passed over the roof of the cottage now. It screeched again.

'Something's in *pain*,' the mother said, screwing up her face.

'Nonsense,' said the father. 'It's the hot water tank letting off steam. I told you to switch it off before we sat down to supper.'

Before dawn, the veil of misty cloud had thickened and the first big drops of heavy summer rain had splattered on to the curved tiles of the church tower. The owl, sensing the coming of rain, had hunted with fierce determination. He had eaten three voles and a couple of field mice and now he slept, satisfied, in the tower.

The rain had cleared by the time the sun rose but heavy clouds covered the sky.

'Just my luck,' the woman grumbled, standing at the door of the house. 'Rain in August! I bet it isn't raining at the seaside.'

Fitful sunshine came and went throughout the day but the rain held off. The windows of the old house, their panes still dim with dust and cobwebs, were flung open. From inside came a constant banging of brooms and splashing of water and the sound of voices calling from room to room. In the early afternoon, the man went away in the car and returned an hour later with a small packet in his hand.

The owl dozed as best he could. He opened his eyes once or twice and saw the children put out a saucer of milk for the cat, then he observed the man squatting at the corner of the house, poking something into the mouse hole there. A few minutes later, the woman came out through the door, a bucket in her hand. She tipped its contents on to the pile of rubbish that was growing by the gate. She noticed her children's legs dangling from the lower branches of the apple tree.

'Come down out of there at once,' she scolded. 'You'll get filthy. And watch what you touch. Your father's put poison down for the mice.'

'I know. We saw him,' said the boy.

'You told us he was going to anyway,' the girl said. 'Twice.'

At dusk, heavy clouds rolled in from the west and it began to rain again in earnest. The dry earth of the garden drank in the water, and when it could absorb no more, rivulets made channels through the dust, and puddles formed on the path. The cat jumped up on to the ledge of a lighted window and mewed raucously. The cottage door was opened abruptly and it trotted inside.

The owl watched and waited. He couldn't hunt in the rain. Once his feathers were waterlogged he would be unable to fly and the chill of the night would make him dangerously cold. He concentrated the formidable power of his eyes on the floor of the belfry, his ears cocked for the telltale scrabble of little clawed feet. An unwary mouse occasionally came up this far, but none had lived to show their friends the way. That night, as usual, none came.

When dawn came, the rain began to ease and the sun rose into a clear sky. The man opened a window and called to his wife.

'Come and have a look,' he said. 'I told you it would be better after the rain. It was a lovely garden in my father's day. Fruit bushes, old-fasioned flowers – once we've got rid of the weeds . . .'

'You're not seriously suggesting we should take up gardening!' the woman said with a laugh. 'It's not exactly my idea of a summer holiday. Anyway, all this vegetation encourages the mice. Can't we pave the whole lot over and be done with it?'

'I suppose you're right.' The man sighed. 'It's a pity though.'

He closed the window.

The rain had freshened the air, and though the sun shone in a cloudless sky all day, the oppressive heat had gone.

By the evening, the owl was desperate with hunger. He waited impatiently for darkness to fall, sidling along the rafter and back again. He shook out his feathers and smoothed them with short strokes of his beak, making them fit for the night's work ahead.

At last the red glow in the western sky disappeared. The owl fluttered to the mullion and perched on the sill, ready to take flight towards the fields below the village.

A faint sound caught his ear. He focussed his eyes. Their powerful lenses picked out the movement of a small creature coming out of the hole by the corner of the house where the man had been busy yesterday.

The owl surveyed the garden. There was no sign of the cat.

He could see the mouse more clearly now. It was moving strangely. Usually, it dashed across the open space to the shelter of the straggling blackcurrant bush, whose unpruned branches made a safe haven close to the ground. Now it ran ahead for a few steps, then staggered. It rocked back on its haunches and lurched on again, directionless, towards the dangerous open ground of the path.

The owl could not resist the temptation. One quick swoop and the meal he longed for would be his. He opened his wings and plunged noiselessly down through the air towards his prey.

At that very moment, when his talons were already stretched out towards the mouse's quivering back and his beak was poised for the strike, the cat came round the corner of the house. It felt the owl's presence like a deadly insult. The garden was *its* territory. It must at all costs keep its enemy away.

With a furious hiss, it launched itself at the owl. He fluttered just out of reach, raising his talons to defend himself. The meal he so desperately needed was still inexplicably within reach. The mouse had not run away. It stood nearby, rocking backwards and forwards, seemingly blind and deaf to everything around it.

The owl's blood was up now. He fluffed out his feathers menacingly, determined to have the mouse, determined suddenly to show his rival once and for all that he was lord of the garden. He let out a screech that made the cat's eyes flare open and the hackles rise along its back. Then he dived. His wings flapped furiously, his beak stabbed, his talons slashed. The cat stood its ground, its lips drawn back in a lion-like snarl, its tail lashing from side to side. It struck back at the owl with a violent assault of teeth and claws.

For a moment, they seemed to be one creature, a spinning mass of pale feathers and black fur, the owl's scream and the cat's snarl almost merging into one sound. And then it was over. The owl had had enough. He rose suddenly into the air, lifting himself just in time out of reach of the cat's mortal strike, then he flapped slowly back up to the safety of his tower.

The cat watched him, still hissing savagely, its body still arched in rage, then a movement from the mouse caught its eye. Triumphantly it pounced, and holding the small body down with one paw, began to eat it.

The owl sat exhausted in the mullion facing out into the night. Bleeding from his wounds, he swayed in the chill night breeze, dazed with pain and hunger. He was almost ready to give up, to stay rooted to his old home until hunger and weakness made him fall from his perch, but a sudden memory came to him of the fat vole he had fed on two nights ago, in the hedgerow by the farm. With the last of his strength, he took off, using the wind to support him, spending as little of his fading energy as he could.

He landed on the dead branch of an oak tree in the corner of the field and within a few minutes felt his confidence return. The voles and shrews, themselves made reckless with hunger after two nights of rain, were running boldly round the harvested field, nibbling at the last few ears of wheat left on the ground.

In quick succession, the owl killed and ate five voles. He returned to his branch, then, without a backwards glance at the church tower on the hill, he set off, flying strongly now, for the farm across the valley. There might be a perch for him there, where he could rest during the day. He would look about, and find a new home. With luck, if he searched far enough afield, he might find a new mate as well.

Five more poisoned mice staggered out of the hole that night. The cat killed and ate them all. In the morning, the children found its body, still warm, stretched out on the doorstep of the cottage.

The Most Precious Thing

A traditional tale from England

There was once a rich man who had three daughters. One day, he said to them, 'How much do you love me, my dears?'

'Oh my darling Father,' said the first. 'I love you as much as I love my life.'

'That's good,' her father answered, and he gave her a pearl necklace.

'And I love you better than the whole world,' said the second daughter.

'Very good,' said her father, and he gave her a gold bracelet.

The youngest daughter thought hard, and at last she said, 'Dear Father, I love you as much as salt.'

Her father was very angry.

'Salt? That nasty, common stuff?' he shouted. 'I can see that you don't love me at all. You are not my daughter any longer!'

He drove her out of the house, and shut the door in her face.

The poor girl wandered about for many a long year, cold and hungry, until at last the fairies found her and took her in.

One day, as she walked through the woods, listening to

the birdsong, a prince rode by on his horse. He fell in love with her at once, and asked her to marry him. He was so good and handsome that she loved him too, and so the wedding was arranged. Invitations were sent out to all the great men of the country and when the rich man received his, he accepted it gladly, though he did not know that the bride was his own daughter.

At the palace, the cooks were preparing a great banquet for the wedding.

'Please,' the girl said to them, 'don't add salt to any of the dishes.'

The cooks were surprised, but they did as she asked.

The wedding took place with great pomp and ceremony. The bride sat in the place of honour, her veil still covering her face, as the guests sat down to eat.

'But there's no salt in this food!' they cried, and they put down their spoons in disgust.

The bride's father hid his face in his hands and wept.

'Salt is the most precious thing in the world,' he said, 'as my own dear daughter tried to tell me. But I drove her away and shut the door in her face, and now she is lost to me forever.'

'Not lost, dear Father. I am here,' the bride said, taking off her veil, and she went up to her father and embraced him.

From that day on, they both lived happily, and never again doubted each other's love.

Why the Sea is Salty

Once upon a time, there were two brothers. One was very rich. His round hut was big and newly thatched, and his stockade was full of cows and sheep. His grain stores were full, and his jars brimmed over with butter and honey.

The other brother was very poor. His hut was small and the thatch was ragged. There were no cows and sheep in his stockade. His grain stores and his jars were empty.

One evening, the poor man's wife said to him, 'Tomorrow is a holiday. Everybody will be feasting on the richest food until they can eat no more. But we have nothing. Our children are starving. Go and ask your brother to give us a little bread, or we will all die.'

So the poor man went to visit his rich brother.

'Dear brother,' he said. 'My wife and I are very poor. We have nothing to eat. Tomorrow is a holiday, and you'll eat a big meal with your family. Please give me a little bread, or my wife and children will die.'

The rich man disliked poor people. He disapproved of beggars, and wanted to keep everything for himself. He stared at his brother haughtily.

'Why do you always beg me for food?' he complained. 'You came last year and the year before. Listen, I'll be very kind to you today. I'll give you a sheep. But don't come back next year. I'll never give you anything again.'

His poor brother thanked him and took the sheep. Then he turned to go.

It was a long way home. The path wound through a deep, dark forest. The man walked fast, but the sun was already low in the sky. Soon, night fell. The man was afraid, but he kept on walking.

I must get home tonight, he thought. I must take this sheep to my poor wife before the holiday begins.

Suddenly, he stopped. In the dim light, he could see a little old man, sitting at the side of the road. The poor man was afraid, but the old man smiled at him.

'Good evening, friend,' he said politely. 'You're out very late. Aren't you afraid to be walking alone in this wild forest? The leopards and hyenas are out hunting already. They'll soon make a meal of you.'

'Oh sir,' said the poor man. 'I have to get home tonight. I'm taking this sheep to my dear wife and children. Tomorrow's a feast day, and we'll kill it and give it to our children to eat. After it's gone we must all die, because we're very poor, and we'll have nothing else to eat.'

'Nothing else to eat?' the old man repeated. 'Then listen to me, my friend. Go down this path into the valley. It will take you into the middle of the forest. You'll find a magnificent palace there. The palace servants will try to buy your sheep for tomorrow's feast. They'll offer you a lot of money. But don't sell it. Look around you. You'll see an old grinding stone beside the door. Say to them, "I don't want money. Give me that old grinding stone, and you can have my sheep." '

'What?' said the poor man. 'But I can't sell my sheep for a grinding stone! My wife and children are hungry. They can't eat a grinding stone.'

'Do what I say,' said the old man. 'You won't be sorry. Give them your sheep and take the grinding stone. Bring it back here to me. I'll tell you what to do next.'

The poor man looked at him.

I don't understand, he thought. But this old man looks kind and trustworthy. Perhaps he means to do me good.

So the poor man went down the path into the middle of the forest. There, to his amazement, stood a magnificent palace. The servants by the gate saw him, and ran out to meet him.

'Oh sir,' they said. 'That is a fine sheep. Will you sell it to us? Tomorrow is a holiday and we don't have any meat. We'll give you a lot of money for it.'

The poor man looked round. He saw the grinding stone beside the door. It was old and chipped and dirty.

'I don't want any money. I'll give you my sheep if you'll give me that grinding stone.'

The servants laughed at him.

'You want that old grinding stone? We don't want it. Take it!'

So the poor man gave them his sheep. He picked up the grinding stone and began to walk up the path again.

Oh, he thought. What a fool I am. I had a big fat sheep and I sold it for this old grinding stone. My wife will be angry with me and my poor little children will cry. We'll have nothing to eat for the holiday, and soon we'll all be dead. That little old man was just trying to trick me. Why did I listen to him? Why?

Soon the poor man came back to the top of the path. The little old man was still sitting there.

'Well done, my friend!' he said. 'You've got the grinding stone. Now, listen to me and you and your family will never go hungry again. When you want something, say to your grinding stone, "Grind, stone, grind." The grinding stone will start to grind. It will give you whatever you want. But when you have enough, you must make it stop. Don't speak to it. Just touch it, and it will stop.'

The poor man thanked him, and hurried back to his house. His wife was waiting for him.

'Husband! Did you see your brother? Did he give you some food for us?'

The poor man could not look at his wife.

'Yes. I saw him. He gave me a sheep.'

His wife laughed with delight.

'A sheep? Where is it?'

Her husband shook his head.

'I – I haven't got it. I sold it.'

'You sold it? Why?' demanded his wife. 'How much money did you get for it?'

'I didn't get any money. I got this grinding stone. Now, wife, don't be angry. This is a magic stone. It'll give us everything we want, and we'll never be hungry again.'

His wife began to shout at him, and his children began to cry, but the man said, 'Be quiet. Wait, and watch.'

He put the grinding stone down on the ground and said, 'Grind, stone, grind. Give my family a feast for the holiday.'

At once, the stone began to turn. Immediately there was a table in the middle of the room and on it was a wonderful meal. Baskets of fresh pancakes gently steamed, and bowls were filled to the brim with spicy stews. Glass flagons of honey mead glowed yellow in the firelight, and succulent fruits lay piled at the side. When the table was so full that it could hold no more, the man touched the grinding stone, and it stopped turning.

'I don't understand it!' said the wife. 'Where did all this food come from?'

'From the magic grinding stone,' her husband told her. 'But don't tell anyone about it. It's a secret.'

The poor man and his wife were very happy, and their children's eyes were wide with wonder. They had enough food to eat for the first time in their lives. They finished everything on the table, then went to bed, and slept well.

A few days later, the poor man invited his brother and all his friends to a meal at his house. The grinding stone turned and turned, and delicious dishes of meat and pancakes soon stood on the table.

The rich brother was very surprised.

'Last week you had nothing,' he said, 'and you came to my house to beg for a piece of bread. Where did all this food come from?'

'I found it,' his brother said, and he refused to tell his secret.

But his brother asked him again and again.

'Tell me! Please tell me,' he said. 'I'm your brother, after all. I always helped you when you came to me. Last week I even gave you a sheep.'

So at last the poor man told his brother about the little old man in the forest, and the palace, and the magic grinding stone.

The rich brother was unhappy now.

I want that grinding stone, he thought. I must have it. My brother must give it to me!

He came back to his brother's house every day, and would not leave him in peace.

'Sell me your grinding stone,' he said again and again. 'I'll give you a lot of money for it.'

At last his poor brother, ground down by his pleading, agreed.

'Come back again after the harvest. I'll sell it to you then.'

The poor brother kept the grinding stone at work from morning to night. He asked it for all the things he wanted, and the grinding stone gave them to him. Now his stores were full of grain, and his jars brimmed over with butter and honey. He had cows and sheep and goats in his stockade, and his wife and children had new clothes and shoes.

After the harvest, the rich brother came back.

'Give me the grinding stone now,' he demanded. 'I'll pay you later. I don't have the money today.'

The poor man knew his brother well.

He'll never pay me, he thought, but he still gave the stone to his rich brother.

'Listen,' he told him. 'When you want something, say to the stone, "Grind, stone, grind." '

But he didn't tell his brother how to stop the stone.

The rich man ran back to his house. He was very happy.

I must keep the secret of the grinding stone, he told himself. I won't tell it to anybody. And he hid the stone in his house.

The next day, he said to his wife, 'Go out and work with the servants in the fields today. I'll stay at home and cook the dinner. Then I'll bring it out to you.'

His wife was very surprised, but she obeyed her husband. She called the servants and went to the fields with them.

At once, the rich man brought out the stone. He put it on the ground and said, 'Grind, stone, grind. Give me milk.'

The grinding stone began to grind. Soon all the pots in the house were full of milk.

'That's enough. You can stop now,' the rich man said, but the grinding stone didn't stop. It made more and more milk.

'Stop!' shouted the man. 'Stop!'

The grinding stone went on turning. The milk ran on to the floor and pushed open the door. It began to run down the road. It carried the rich man out with it. He was very angry.

'Stop, you stupid grinding stone! Stop!' he shouted.

All this time, the rich man's wife and servants were working in the fields.

Where's my husband? the woman thought. He should have brought our dinner out to us by now. Perhaps he needs my help.

She called the servants, and they all began to hurry home. When they were near the house, they heard shouts and screams. There, on the road, was a river of milk, and in the middle of the river was the rich man. The milk was nearly over his head, and he held the grinding stone in his hands.

'Wife! Help me, quickly!' he called out. 'Fetch my brother! This magic is too strong for me.'

His wife ran to her brother-in-law's house.

'Come quickly, and help your brother! He's drowning in a river of milk!'

The poor brother smiled.

'My brother bought the grinding stone from me. But he never gave me the money for it. He must pay me or I won't help him.'

'He'll pay! He'll pay!' cried the rich man's wife.

She ran back to her house and fetched the money, and gave it to her brother-in-law. He touched the grinding stone and it stopped turning. At once the milk stopped running.

'Take your grinding stone,' the rich man said to his brother. 'I never want to see it again!'

The poor man went home with the grinding stone, and with his pockets full of money. He was a rich man now. He bought a big, beautiful house, and he and his family had everything they wanted.

The man with the grinding stone soon became famous. People came to visit him from all over Ethiopia. They wanted to see his grinding stone and admire his riches.

One day, a man from Gambella in the deep south west came to see him. He had some boats on the Baro River.

'My friend,' he said, 'please will you lend me your grinding stone? I'll keep it only for a short time, and then I'll give it back to you. I'll ask the grinding stone to make salt, which I'll carry up and down the river, and sell it from my boats. Salt fetches a good price and I'll make a lot of money.'

The man with the grinding stone listened kindly to the man from Gambella, and he agreed to lend him his stone.

'When you want salt,' he said to him, 'say to the stone, "Grind, stone, grind." '

The man from Gambella was very happy. He picked up the stone and ran away with it.

'Wait!' the stone's owner called out after him. 'You don't know how to stop it!'

But the man from Gambella was too impatient. He didn't stop to listen. He wanted to start making salt at once.

He hurried back to Gambella, and jumped into one of his boats.

'Grind, stone, grind,' he commanded. 'Fill my boat with salt.'

At once, the stone began to turn. Soon, salt was running down into the boat. The man was very happy.

I'm rich! Rich! he thought.

The stone turned and turned. Soon, the boat was full.

'Stop,' cried the man. 'There's enough salt now.'

But the grinding stone turned on and on, faster and faster. The boat began to break up under the man's feet.

'Stop!' he shouted. 'Or the boat will sink!'

The grinding stone didn't stop. The boat broke into two pieces and sank into the water. The grinding stone sank too, down to the bottom of the river.

The water carried the grinding stone down the Baro River, and into the Nile, and the Nile carried it out into the sea. There lies the grinding stone to this very day, turning and turning, making salt, far down below at the bottom of the deep blue sea.

Deep Sea and Dry Land

A North American Story

Once there was no land. Only a vast ocean existed, with the sky above it. Fish, seabirds and water-loving animals lived in the ocean, while Sky People inhabited the sky.

One day, by a terrible accident, the daughter of the Sky Chief fell through a hole in the sky. As she fell, she screamed. Turtle heard her cries and called to the other creatures. Two swans flew up at once, and caught the Sky Chief's daughter in their strong white wings. They hovered, holding her between them.

'Help us, Turtle!' they cried. 'She's too heavy for us! We can't hold her for long!'

Turtle looked at the other animals who had clustered round.

'One of you must dive to the bottom of the sea,' he said, 'and bring me some mud so that I can make dry land.'

Otter tried first. He plunged down into the dark cold regions of the ocean, further and further, deeper and deeper, but before he could reach the bottom his breath ran out and, nearly bursting, he swam up to the surface again.

'Hurry!' the swans were calling. 'We can't hold her much longer!'

Beaver was the next to try, but for him, too, the ocean

133

was too deep. He rose to the surface, gasping for air.

'I'll go,' croaked Toad.

He puffed himself up with air, and plunged. Down and down he went, his small legs pumping through the water. At last he reached the bottom, scooped a little mud up in his mouth and with the last of his strength swam up to the surface again. Half dead with exhaustion, he spat the mud out on to Turtle's broad back, then floated, panting, with his eyes half closed.

The tiny patch of mud began to spread. It rolled outwards, forwards, sideways, on and on, covering Turtle's vast shell, rising into mountains and falling into valleys, and the swans, their tired wings creaking, landed at last, setting the Sky Chief's daughter gently down on the newly formed land.

Turtle lives beneath us still, holding the land on his back. Most of the time he sleeps, but sometimes he wakes, and moves, and then the earth quakes beneath our feet.

It was almost totally dark in the box. The young otter trembled, crouching in a corner. Until today she had always felt safe in this warm familiar nest. She and her twin brother had lain in it curled up together to sleep, ever since they had been separated from their mother and brought to the big enclosure to live on their own.

But there was no sense of safety now. Everything was strange and frightening.

The trouble had started hours ago. The little otter and her brother had been sleeping, as they usually did all through the day, when she had been woken by the sound of human feet approaching, and human voices talking nearby. Then, with a suddenness that had made her tense up with fear and lurch against her brother, their sleeping box had started moving. It had risen into the air, and then there had been a grating sound as it was slid on to a hard surface. After that came a clanking as if a metal door was closing.

The otter had recognised the sound of a car engine. She had seen cars many times, especially the old Land Rover which came twice a day to the enclosure, bringing food and fresh water, but she had never heard one so close before. She hunkered down, bracing herself, as the noise of the engine continued. She could hear the sound of human voices now, very close, and could smell the human smell too, mixed up with other, unknown scents of oil, and old upholstery, and staleness.

'Are you sure they're all right back there?' the girl in the passenger seat was saying. 'I mean they won't suffocate or anything, will they?'

'They're fine. Don't fuss,' the man's voice said, and then the vehicle swung round a sharp corner, and the otters skittered nervously, their noses and whiskers twitching with fear.

The noise of the engine was cut, and suddenly the box was moving again, swinging up and down, and the human smell was overpowering and frighteningly near. Then the movement stopped as the box was set down, and there came the sound of car doors slamming, and the noise of the engine faded away into the distance.

The otters shifted about uneasily inside their box. Strange sensations were penetrating through its wooden walls. The constant low hum of a busy road, near which they had lived all their lives, was suddenly absent. There were new sounds: harsh cawings from a rookery, and the drumming of a woodpecker on a tree. And instead of the familiar scent of the old pond, where as cubs they had learned to dive and swim, there was the smell of new water, running water, a river, intriguing but strange.

The young otter's brother, who had been turning restlessly in the enclosed space, began to creep down the curved entrance tunnel attached to the side of the box. He halted just inside it, and she knew he was looking out, sniffing the air, alert for danger.

Then he was gone. One minute his bulk was blocking out the daylight, and the next there was only a square of brightness. Daringly, she approached the entrance herself and peered out, her whiskers quivering, alert to every sound and smell.

She saw that she was in a new enclosure, much smaller than the old one. Their box had been set down under a tree, around which grass stretched out towards an encircling fence. Her brother was nowhere to be seen, but she could hear him. Crunching noises were coming from inside another box nearby. He was eating.

The thought of food gave her courage and, with one more wary look round, she launched herself out of the tunnel and ran across the open ground towards the feeding box.

Her brother darted out of it when he heard her coming. He was holding a big piece of fish in his mouth.

He sat back on his haunches in the open air, held the fish in his paws and bit off mouthfuls, tilting his head sideways as he chewed.

She nosed her way into the feeding box. There was plenty of food left in the dish. She picked up another piece and, her courage rising, ran outside with it too and began to eat.

On the hill some way away, the girl and her father were watching through binoculars.

'They've found the food,' the girl said. 'Look, they're eating.'

The meal had given the otters confidence. Cat-like, they cleaned themselves, licking their faces, working down the white fur on their bellies, twisting their brown heads round to nibble at their backs and tails.

They began to explore. The male found the water trough first. He nosed round it, but his sister, more adventurous for once, was attracted by the smell of the river nearby. She made for the fence and put out a paw to test its strength before trying to wriggle through.

A painful buzz of electricity shot through her, making her jump backwards and chitter with fright. She sniffed at the wire, but didn't dare touch it again. Slowly, she trotted back to the trough, and her brother.

The man lowered his binoculars and grunted with satisfaction.

'The electric fence is working. They won't try getting past that again.'

★ ★ ★

Days passed. At first the otters moved cautiously round their pen, cocking their heads to listen to every unfamiliar sound, calling anxiously when they were momentarily out of sight of each other. As they learned their new territory they became more confident. They began to play, diving into their water trough, performing acrobatics in its confined space, chasing each other over the grass, then touching noses, snatching up fallen leaves and feathers and playing tug-of-war.

The dish in the food box was filled with fresh fish and meat every day. They didn't try to touch the fence again.

On the tenth day, when the man and the girl came with food, the otters hid as usual in their sleeping box. The humans left the enclosure, shutting the gate securely behind them.

'They're used to the place now. We'll do it tonight,' the man said.

'Are you sure?'

'Yes. Come on.'

He climbed into the Land Rover, but the girl lingered, hoping to see a brown whiskered muzzle or a questing paw at the entrance to the box. Nothing appeared. With a long backward glance, she climbed into the passenger seat and the Land Rover drove away.

In the late twilight of that summer's night, the man and the girl came back. The otters had been playing in the water trough, twisting and doubling expertly between its narrow walls. They scrambled out when they heard the car in the distance, shook water off their thick coats in a shower of bright drops, then rolled in the grass to dry themselves. They were curled up together in their box before the tread of feet approached.

Usually, the people came and went quickly, and when they had gone, food was lying in the dish in the food box, but something else was happening tonight. Their voices came from the far end of the enclosure, where the smell of water was strongest.

'Don't touch it yet. I'm not sure if the current's switched off,' the man was saying.

There were more confused sounds, and then he spoke again.

'It's all right now. You can unhook the wire and roll it up.'

The otters heard the click of metal against metal, and a continuous trampling of feet. The man's heavier steps moved away towards the car. The door opened and closed and the engine started. The girl lingered. She spoke again, softly.

'Good luck. I hope you make it out there.'

The otters waited, as they always did, for the sound of the car to die away. Then they bundled joyfully out of their sleeping box, confident that food would be waiting for them.

They hesitated, aware at once that something was different.

The wire that had hurt them when they'd touched it, had gone.

The young male loped over to the place where it had been, his heavy, rudder-like tail trailing across the grass. He stopped, ears pricked, nose a-twitch, searching out every tiny sign of change.

His sister joined him. Together they sniffed cautiously about, interpreting scents, making sure that the smell of the painful wire had gone. Their long white whiskers delicately felt for every leaf and bump in the ground, checking for strange objects.

Nothing seemed to be amiss. There was no sign of danger.

Curiosity and fear fought inside each of them for a long moment. The smell of new water won.

A tangle of thickly growing wild flowers – tall willow herb and meadowsweet – lay between them and the river. They began to move through the undergrowth, sensitive paws outstretched to feel the way.

And then they were on the grassy bank of the broad, gently flowing stream, looking down into its depths. For a while they sidled along the edge, smelling and testing, then the lure of the water drew them in. One after another they dived, and the welcoming water closed over them.

It was almost completely dark now, but their eyes, better able to see underwater than through air, could still pick out the shape of the stones on the stream bed and a dark mass of weed that hugged a curve of the bank.

The young female was aware of a thousand sensations she had never known before. The water in her home

141

pond, where she had grown up, had been still and dark. Here the water was moving, and as she lay in it, it rippled along her sleek body like a living thing. The current alarmed her for a moment, but then she began to work against it, kicking with her powerful back paws, and in doing so her rader-like whiskers sensed a little creature darting by. She turned and snapped at it.

The stickleback was the first food she had ever hunted for herself. She chewed and swallowed and liked it. The taste of it excited her and she began to nose about more purposefully.

Ahead, her brother's shape loomed. She felt the need to be close to him and swam at him, straight as an arrow, tucking her paws into her body as she came up underneath him, and pushed at him playfully.

Her tail dislodged a stone, and a good-sized fish darted out from underneath it. Both otters lunged for it, but it shot away from them. They plunged after it, but confused by the current and the fish's erratic movements, they let it get away.

All night, the two creatures explored, now in the river and now on the bank. They found and ate a couple of frogs each, but the bigger prey still escaped their inexperienced grasp.

Tired at last, they circled back to their old enclosure and took the food from the dish, their appetites sharpened by the intense activity of the last few hours. They tussled over the biggest piece, baring their teeth angrily at each other, but the bigger male soon won, and ran off to eat it alone.

With new energy, and eager with curiosity and excitement, they trotted back to the water. They plunged in, and swam upstream. Already used to the current, they moved together, twin dark streaks, their backs mounding through the water. Then they lay close under the surface, eyes and noses only showing, and disappeared at last into the depths, to skim confidently close to the river bed.

This time they explored much further, and when the birds in a patch of woodland by the bank broke out into the dawn chorus, they were already a couple of miles downstream. They climbed out of the water and dried themselves, then pattered around. They took cover once when a badger lumbered past on his dawn return to his sett, and again when a pheasant rose up unexpectedly in front of them with a wild whirring of wings. Nothing else disturbed them.

They found a resting place in the shadow of a low branch, biting down some ragged-Robin flowers and a clump of reeds to make a couch. They lay down, snuggling against each other as they always had done since the day they were born. They slept.

Back at the enclosure, the man and the girl had come early, bringing fresh food with them. The girl gingerly lifted the lid of the sleeping box and peeped inside.

'They've gone,' she said, her excitement mixed with disappointment.

'They'll come back when they're hungry,' said her father, filling the dish and pushing it into the feeding box.

On their second night of freedom the female otter felt a new sensation on the end of her whiskers. Turning more deftly this time, she caught a small eel in her jaws. She swam with it to the river bank, killed it with a bite to the head, and ate it greedily. She liked it more than any other food she had ever eaten.

She was learning to hunt efficiently now, learning to sense the movement of living things in the water, to follow cunningly and pounce quickly.

She was taking control of her new territory too, marking it with her droppings and making it her own. Her brother ranged further, up and down the stream. She was content to spend time alone.

On the fifth night after their release, the two otters met at the feeding box in the old enclosure, more from habit than from hunger. They had both hunted well, feasting on frogs. The male had nearly caught a moorhen, snatching at the webbed foot that dangled down temptingly from the surface of the water.

During the following day, they lay curled up together as they had always done. The male was the first to leave. He had marked out a strip of the upper stream as his territory, and he was eager to return to it. He had caught the scent of a female otter. He found it strange and exciting.

His sister had found a good place for herself under the roots of a tree, which grew close by the water's edge.

She had already begun to dig out a den with her strong-clawed paws.

Neither of them returned to the food box again.

Months passed. The days grew shorter. Blackberries ripened in the hedges and the pink flowers of the willow herb turned to wisps of white fluff. Later, it grew frosty, and the bare twigs rattled in the cold wind.

Spring arrived early the next year. Rain filled the stream to the brim, and brought out the catkins to flutter in the breeze.

Every day, the man picked up the girl from school in the old farm jeep. Every day they stopped on the bridge above the stream, and got out, leaning on the parapet to look down into the water.

'They're about somewhere,' the man said, one day in May. 'There are always fresh droppings here, under the bridge.'

'Do you think they're still together?' said the girl.

'I doubt it. They'll need different territories if they're to breed. Brothers and sisters don't usually stay together. We'll have to hope they've met the otters that were released higher up last year.'

The girl suddenly stiffened and pointed down into the water. A long line of bubbles was rising through the water, though not even the slightest ripple showed on the surface.

'Yes,' the man whispered. 'It could be. Yes.'

The otter reached the bank. Her head, satiny with

wetness, bobbed up suddenly, breaking the surface. She scrambled out onto the grass and shook herself. The humans froze, scarcely daring to breathe.

Then the water broke again, and a smaller head appeared, followed by another.

'Cubs!' the girl breathed. 'She's got cubs!'

Her slight movement had alerted the otter. With a sinuous movement she disappeared into the undergrowth, and the cubs whisked themselves into hiding behind her.

The girl's eyes were shining.

'We've done it!' she said. 'We've brought them back!'

Her father hugged her.

'I never thought I'd see the day,' he said. 'There were otters all along the river here when I was a boy. I thought they'd been wiped out for good. But they'll be fine now. They're breeding. They've truly come home.'